Dearest Anna
Your own copy
"Long may yer lum reek!"
All my love, Billy xxx

PAINFUL

BAD DAY BOOKS

This is a work of fiction. Names, characters, places, and incidents are either the product of the author's imagination or are used fictitiously. Any resemblance to actual persons, living or dead, events, or locales is entirely coincidental.

Copyright © Billy Hamon

All rights reserved. No part of this book may be reproduced or used in any matter without written permission of the copyright owner except for the use of quotations in a book review.

First paperback edition November 2021

Book design by Billy Hamon

Billy Hamon was delivered in the front room of 4 Mayo Rd, Walton-on-Thames, by a midwife who marvelled at his amazing eyes. According to his mum he could roller-skate at one, read and write by the age of two, and miraculously see at birth.

After failing all his GCSE's he decided to become a penniless writer. His first job was on a children's TV series entitled *Pipkins*, writing for such luminary characters as Hartley Hare, Tortoise, Pig and Topov The Monkey. His first stage play *Grafters* was performed at the Hampstead Theatre, London, for which he won the Evening Standard Most Promising Playwright Award. Unable to follow it up, he became a regular writer on *Eastenders*, *Casualty*, *Boon* and *Soldier Soldier* as well as his own original series for Channel 4 which no one saw.

He has two lovely children, Paul and Esther, who he adores and regards as his best friends. He's been married three times and at least two of his wives refuse to speak to him.

In spite of all his limited success he remains penniless, thus fulfilling his adolescent dream.

PAINFUL

Special thanks to my lovely friend Louis for being a brilliant editor and turning it into something readable.

PAINFUL

By the same author

GREAT RECIPES FOR POTHEADS LIVING ON THEIR OWN BY DICKHEAD DAVE

For Choochie

PAINFUL

Based on true events.

PAINFUL

PART ONE

A Toe In The Water

PAINFUL

1

Most people view life as horizontal, whereas mystics and sages see it as vertical. I tend to think of it as a road map written by an idiot. You can't see the bumps or the potholes ahead, and just when you think you're almost there that great satnav in the sky decides to surprise you with a speed hump.

I'd played a round of golf with a so-called 'friend' of mine, Steve Fisher, who wasn't exactly my cup of tea. Essex wide boy made good. Loud, crass, crude, a complete narcissist who bragged about everything whether it was true or not. He assumed because he was good-looking he could get away with it and usually did. He was also one of life's natural born cheats. He couldn't help himself. He cheated in business, he cheated at golf, and of course he cheated on his wife, *constantly*, without guilt or remorse. Apart from that he was an okay bloke, I suppose. At least he kept in touch and was always up for 18 holes.

I've always thought you can tell a lot about a person from the way they play golf. Steve's game was brash and erratic. He just wanted to smash the ball as hard as he could no matter where he was on the fairway. Consequently his shots would often go wildly off-course, either landing in the rough or disappearing into the trees. He'd then totally lose it and start smacking his club on the ground like a tempestuous teenager, often breaking it in half. Then he'd storm off in a huff and search for the ball which was nowhere to be seen. Strangely enough, though, he always seemed to find it.

PAINFUL

Of course, when he hit it correctly it went for miles, giving him the chance of a birdie, an eagle, or even an albatross. Then he'd get on the green and completely balls it up with his putting which was as erratic as his sex life.

Now for those of you who don't play golf, a birdie is very good, an eagle is brilliant, and an albatross is out of this world. Even pros rarely get an albatross. It's the equivalent of a hole in one on a par 4. A par is good, a bogie is just about bearable, but a double and a triple bogie are *disastrous*! And anything over that you might as well take up knitting. Steve, however, somehow always managed to get a par or at *most* a bogie even when I'd seen him take eight shots getting out of a bunker. I never said anything. What was the point? The only one he was cheating was himself. But his ego couldn't allow him to lose.

My game was safe, steady and accurate. I knew the right club to choose and knew roughly how far it would go and where it would land. I never tried to hit it too hard or do anything fancy, just a nice easy half-swing off the tee, another safety shot from the fairway, a little chip onto the green, and then a cool, calm putt into the hole. My putting was the best part of my game, straight and consistent, often saving the old scorecard. Okay, I wasn't Seve Ballesteros, but I didn't have to be. I nearly always went round in a decent 14-over, the same as my handicap, which meant I was actually on-par, if that makes sense.

I can understand how confusing this must be to all you sports fans who don't follow golf. The object of nearly every other game is to score as many points as possible. Golf is the absolute opposite. A bit like walking backwards for Christmas. Or trying to lose at tennis. Or trying not to score a goal. As someone once said, "It's a terrible way to spoil a good stroll."

So what did my game say about me? Boring? Predictable? Incapable of taking risks? Yes, probably, all of those. But it also said I was honest, reliable and trustworthy. Which was, I suppose, why Yvette decided to marry me. It certainly wasn't my banter or experimentation in bed.

She was 26, blonde, gorgeous, glamorous and vivacious. She'd been a holiday rep and an underwear model. She was even in one of those awful reality TV shows where they live on some desert island and try to find their perfect match. *Fantasy Beach Hut*, I think it was called, or something similar. Unfortunately it bombed and she never became the reality star she hoped to be.

I met her at the gym where she was working up enough of a sweat to make the average man feel ill. And, boy, did she look good doing it! I'd never seen *anyone* carry off a leotard like that! Her breasts virtually popped out and said 'hi' before *she* did. And I didn't have to do anything, which was good because I'm actually quite shy and *terrible* at the old chat-up lines. She saw me, smiled, and invited me for a drink. That night we slept together.

I've never been much on the old sex front. There always seemed more important things to think about. But Yvette – how can I put it without sounding discourteous – Yvette was rather adept in the old sack. She *loved* it! And lots of it. But I won't go into details as that would be ungentlemanly. All I'll say is her favourite position was something called the 'reverse cowgirl', which sounded rather dangerous to me as I'd never had riding lessons. Fortunately I was the horse.

PAINFUL

She soon moved in and then decided we should get married. I'd never been married before. Relationships had never really been my thing. I'd had the odd three-to-six month stint, but they never felt particularly essential. I was just as happy staying in with a good book and a glass of chenin blanc.

So, anyway, Steve and I finished our round with him winning, of course, thanks to his dodgy scorecard and bent handicap of 27 which gave him a 13-shot advantage. We were about to go into the clubhouse for our usual aftergame drink when I suddenly changed my mind and said I was going home. I'm not sure why.

Decisions. Why do we make them and who decides if they're right? Us? Or some higher power, like God, karma, destiny or fate? Or is it just a series of haphazard guesses and clueless calculations?

It was early January, almost 4 o' clock, and already getting dark. We'd only just made the 18th. It had been a lovely crisp winter's day, but now you could feel the cold night air really beginning to bite. And I suddenly got this overwhelming urge to go home and see my new, young, beautiful wife of three months and have a lovely warm kiss and cuddle in front of the fake log fire. It was either that or sit in the clubhouse and watch Steve trying to pull the new barmaid who had to be all of 18. He did everything to get me to stay because, for a start, I always bought the first round (and sometimes the second if he could get away with it), and he also liked an audience, especially when he was chatting-up 18-year-old barmaids. But I was fixed on the idea of getting home early. In fact, I couldn't wait. I got in the Volvo and left the club with no inkling of the life-changing events to come.

One decision leads to another. But can a right decision be followed by a wrong one? Or a wrong decision turn into a right one? Or does a wrong decision *always* lead irrevocably to another wrong one, then another, culminating in one hell of a bad day?

I reached the traffic lights where you either went straight on for the town centre or did a left and drove down a narrow country lane, no lighting and some extremely hazardous bends. The town centre was a 20-mile-an-hour speed limit and would obviously be busy around four o' clock with the school run. The other was a no limit and cut at least ten minutes off the journey. So there was my dilemma – the long way in the light or the quick way in the dark. As I sat there waiting for the lights to change, I must have changed my mind at least a dozen times. *I used to be indecisive but now I wasn't so sure.*

The lights turned green and I suddenly did the left, entering the long, dark, winding lane. And almost immediately I knew, or *sensed,* that it was the wrong decision. *Why*? I don't know. I argued with myself, called it illogical. But I still couldn't shake that feeling. At any time I could have stopped and turned back. But I didn't. I dismissed it and called the missus.

"Hello, darling."

"*Brian*! What a surprise!"

"*Is* it?"

"Thought you'd still be playing golf."

"It's pitch black!" I laughed. "Can't play golf in the pitch black, darling. Can't see the green!"

Yvette laughed with me.

"But aren't you going for a drink with Steve?"

"No, I'm on my way home."

Her voice seemed to change.

"What – *now*?"

"Yes, I'll be home in ten minutes."

She sounded strangely concerned.

"Ten *minutes*?"

"Nine minutes forty-three seconds, according to the satnav."

I *always* called her on the hands-free when I was on my way home. And for a moment I forgot the strange, eerie feeling that something bad was about to happen.

We ended the call and I thought no more about it. I just kept driving into the darkness with the road narrowing either side. It was almost as if I wanted to prod it, poke it, play with it. That thought. It was like my life was doing the rumba with my demise.

At one point I turned on the CD player: 'Moon River' by Henry Mancini from a compilation of romantic love songs entitled *Everything For The Lady* that I'd bought for Yvette.

"Moon River, wider than a mile
I'm crossing you in style someday ...."

Suddenly I see two headlights coming towards me. Full beam. Blinding. Driving too fast. I dipped my lights. Unfortunately the other car didn't.

"Oh, dream maker, you heartbreaker ...."

It gradually dawned on me that it was on the wrong side of the road, coming straight for me, and it wasn't slowing down.

"Wherever you're going I'm going your way ...."

I kept waiting for them to move to their side of the road, but they didn't. By the time I realized they weren't going to, it was too late. It was either a head-on collision or a swerve off the road and into a tree. I chose the tree.

They say accidents happen in slow motion and it's true. Everything stops. Time, thoughts, past and future.

You're in the now because that's all there is. And you almost stand there and watch it happen.

I remember the tree coming towards me, a massive thud, the sound of metal and machine ripping apart, my head and torso being thrown forward, the airbag inflating to lessen the impact. All simultaneously, yet somehow separated by a lifetime. Then nothing. Just silence. Complete, utter, almost immaculate silence. Then seconds that seemed like hours to return to 'ordinary time' and piece together what had happened. There was no pain yet, just shock. My first thought, weirdly, was that the music had stopped. Then I looked around and saw the other car on the opposite side of the road, stopped as if observing me. It was too dark to make out exactly what kind of car it was, but it was small, like a Mini. Then it quickly drove off into the night, never to be seen again.

I suddenly smelt burning and noticed a small fire behind the dashboard. I now moved with speed and urgency. I managed to unclip my seatbelt, throw open the door, and literally fell out onto the grass verge, landing on my back. This was when I realized my legs were smashed. I couldn't feel them until I tried to move them, and then there was this sharp, searing pain that ran from my feet all the way up to my head. And, unbelievably, the CD suddenly started up again.

"Two drifters off to see the world
There's such a lot of world to see ...."

I could now see the smoke pouring out from the engine. I thought it was going to burst into flames at any moment. I managed to pull myself backwards on my elbows until I was a reasonably safe distance away, and that's when the pain *really* kicked in. I couldn't see the damage but I knew it was bad. It felt like both legs had been smashed with a sledgehammer. I reached into my pocket, found my phone, and called for an ambulance. My voice sounded strangely calm and matter-of-fact, as if someone else was saying it.

And that's when I must have passed out.

2

The next thing I remember is lying on an examination table with screens all around, wearing nothing but one of those horrendous hospital gowns that tie at the back and expose your bottom. I could hear a loud beeping sound, there was a needle in my arm, and there seemed to be tubes everywhere. I had vague recollections of the ambulance, people staring down at me, but mostly it was a blur.

I looked down and could now see the full extent of my injuries. It wasn't pretty. I felt like throwing-up. Both legs had turned blue and there was a large gaping wound in one of them. You could almost see the bone. I was just about to pass out again when a lovely young nurse entered.

"Hello, poppet, how's the pain?"

"Starting to throb."

"I'll get you some more pain killers."

"Where am I?"

"You're in Sunningdale Park Hospital, poppet. We're about to take you to X-ray."

"Is my wife here?"

"Your wife? I'm not sure. Maybe she's in the waiting room."

Two men wheeled me to the X-ray department where a tired overworked lady who looked like she'd been there forever positioned the machine and took photos of my legs from several different angles. I remember being conscious of my toenails and cursed myself for not having cut them that morning.

I was then taken to the examination room, a small, sterile, windowless room where the full enormity of what had happened finally hit home. How would I get

PAINFUL

around? What if both legs had to be amputated? Most importantly of all, would I ever be able to play golf again?

The same young nurse entered holding some pills in a paper cup and handed them to me with a drink of water.

"Thank you," I said gratefully and swallowed them while she surveyed the damage.

"How did it happen?"

"I was driving home and a tree got in the way."

"Not to worry, poppet. They'll soon sort you out. The orthopaedist should be here any moment."

She turned and started to leave.

"Is my wife here yet?"

She stopped and turned back and I saw how truly beautiful she really was. She looked like an angel.

"I'll find out for you."

Aah, the good old NHS. Like a lovely warm blanket that wraps itself around you, comforts and protects you whilst ignoring its own aches and pains. An enormous juggernaut still chugging along even though it's clapped-out and in urgent need of an MOT. Even so, I was awfully glad I would have a room to myself thanks to my private health insurance.

The door opened and in came this tall, thin, pale-looking man in a white coat, holding my X-rays. Around the same age as me, rather grey and bland, but well on the way to becoming a full-blown eccentric.

"Well, now, Mr May .... I'm Dr Cox. And guess what?"

I shook my head.

"We're both called Brian. Which means *I'm* a famous TV scientist .... and *you're* the lead guitarist of Queen! And guess what else?"

I shook my head again, clueless.

22

"They're both known for their hair. Which is rather ironic really, isn't it, given that *your* hair is cut short and *I'm* going bald!"

He laughed hysterically. I was speechless. I honestly didn't know what to say.

"So. We've had a bit of an accident, have we?"

"Well .... I have .... *you* haven't."

"Got stung by a wasp, did we?"

"Sorry?"

"Got stung by a wasp? That's what happened to me. Driving along, wasp in the car, stings me in the head, next thing I know I've passed out and smacked into a telegraph pole. Fortunately it had woodworm. The telegraph pole, that is, not the wasp."

I now realized he was completely mad.

"So. We've looked at your X-rays .... and it's not good news, I'm afraid. Both legs have open compound fractures. Do you know what they are?"

I'd already shaken my head so often I was feeling dizzy. Dr Brian Cox, the orthopaedist not the famous TV scientist, obviously liked a bit of patient participation.

"Complicated breaks where the bone has broken through the skin. This is quite serious and needs urgent attention. So we're going to operate to realign the broken bones and possibly insert an internal fixation devise. Do you know what that is?"

"I'm sure you'll tell me."

"Metal plate, rods or screws .... maybe some metal wires .... but we won't really know till we're in there and opened you up. Think of it like a car. You can open the bonnet and have a bit of a poke around, but you wouldn't really expect the mechanic to diagnose the problem until he's taken the engine apart, would you?

Not unless it's something obvious like your big end or distributor cap."

For once I nodded.

"Then after the surgery we'll leave the legs to rest for a while, then providing they're healing okay, it'll be on with the old plaster casts and 6-8 weeks of R and R. Any questions?"

"How was the wasp?" I asked flippantly.

He didn't respond.

3

The next day I was in a private room in The Churchill Suite, akin to a small Holiday Inn, with the staff catering to my every whim. The young pretty nurse was in attendance and I discovered her name was Kimberly, which suited her. The food was excellent too. A choice of kippers, boiled egg or porridge for breakfast, and a three-course meal for lunch. I wasn't, however, exactly hungry. I was too bruised and battered. Both legs were in traction, hoisted up about three feet, making me feel like a dead turkey hanging in a butcher's window. The good news was that I wouldn't lose them.

Suddenly the door opened and in burst Yvette, one of the few times I'd ever seen her without makeup. She was pale, distraught, her eyes were red and her hair lank. She rushed in anxiously.

"Brian! Oh, Brian! Are you alright? Oh, darling, this is *terrible*! What happened?"

I wasn't pleased with her and let her know it.

"What *happened*? I had an *accident*! Twenty four hours ago!"

But Yvette, as usual, immediately spat back like a cornered alley cat.

"Well, there's no need to get shirty, darling! I got here as soon as I could!"

"*Twenty four hours,* Yvette!"

"I couldn't find it! Sunningdale Park Hospital? Who on earth has heard of Sunningdale Park Hospital?"

"But you've got a satnav!"

"It's not working!"

"The internet? Your smartphone? An A to Z?"

PAINFUL

She then went into her tried and tested close-to-tears routine.

"I *rang*! They told me you were asleep and to call back later! Why are you being so horrible? I thought you'd be pleased to see me!"

I had to relent otherwise this would have gone on all night.

"Yes. Of course. Sorry, darling. It's been a bit .... a bit of an emotional time."

"For me too. I hardly slept last night!"

"You poor thing."

"So what's the damage?"

She then noticed my legs for the first time and looked positively repulsed.

"Oh, my God!"

They *did* look like something out of a horror film. There were scars, stitches, the bruises had turned purple, and both legs were now in an external fixation device, a metal frame that's outside the leg and attached through the tissue into the bone.

"Both legs broken," I told her stoically. "Multiple fractures, a metal plate in one, a dozen screws in the other ...."

She cut me off, too nauseated to hear it.

"So what happened exactly?"

"I was driving home and this bloody idiot came racing towards me. Must have been drunk. Doing at least seventy. I swerved to avoid him and hit a tree."

"Did you see the driver?"

"No, his headlights were in my eyes."

"What about his number plate? Did you get his number plate?"

"No, it all happened so fast. Fast and yet .... at the same time slow. Dead slow. Fast *and* slow. Like a Beatles record."

"What about the make of car?"

"No, it was too dark. But I think it was small. A small car. Something like a Mini."

And she suddenly started to cry. *Real* crying, not the fake stuff she did when she couldn't get her own way. True heartbreaking sobs. And I found myself comforting her, holding her hand and speaking reassuringly.

"Don't worry, darling – it'll be alright. I'll be fine. We're okay for money. The new show is doing well. The mortgage is paid up, no outstanding debts. Then there's all the insurance policies I took out when I was eighteen ...."

I'm lying there with two broken legs, recovering from an operation, and *I'm* comforting *her*! But that was Yvette for you – she could wrangle pity from a homeless blind man sleeping in a disused toilet.

"That's not why I'm crying," she snivelled. "I'm crying because .... I'm leaving you."

It took a moment for me to take in what she'd actually said.

"Pardon?"

"I'm leaving you. Sorry, Brian – I know it's not the ideal time. But I realized last night .... when they called me to say you'd been in an accident .... I realized that if you were bedridden .... if you could never walk again .... I wouldn't be able to look after you. I mean, I wouldn't *want* to. It's not in me. And if you can't look after someone when they're bedridden then it can't be right, can it? There must be something wrong. It must mean you don't love them enough. And that's no good for either of us .... *is* it?"

"Who is he?" I suddenly enquired.

She stopped dead in her tracks.

"What?"

"The other man. Who is he?"

She turned ashen.

"What makes you think there's another man?"

"Come off it, Yvette. I know you well enough to know you can't be on your own. What's his *name*?"

She looked like a naughty schoolgirl who'd been caught at the back of the school with her knickers down.

"Paco," she said quietly.

I snickered. I couldn't even muster-up outrage.

"How old?"

"Twenty-two."

"What does he do?"

"He's a personal fitness trainer."

I openly laughed.

"That figures."

"You don't seem .... that shocked."

"Underwear."

"Pardon?"

"You always know when a woman is having an affair when she keeps buying new underwear. I read it in one of your Cosmopolitans. *You've* been buying enough underwear to give Melania Trump a run for her money."

"I'm still very fond of you," she uttered unconvincingly.

"Don't worry – I won't stitch you up in the divorce settlement. I'll be just as generous as I've always been."

She looked as guilty as hell and lowered her eyes, unable to look at me.

"Take care, darling. Look after yourself. Hope you mend okay. Sorry it didn't work out."

And she turned and left as quickly as possible without a backwards glance.

I sat there, bemused, marvelling at the sudden end to our three-month marriage. It felt like the whole thing had been a sort of dream – or nightmare – depending on what side of the bed you were on.

4

As I laid there for the next few days I realized I had no friends, no *real* friends, no one to ask or turn to. Parents dead, two sisters living abroad who I hadn't spoken to for years, and in spite of being what I'd call 'comfortably off' there was nobody close, just acquaintances, business associates. The sort that came and went with the last deal. I was alone with my injuries and the heartbreak of a sham marriage. I'd never felt more abandoned in all my life.

Unexpectedly the door flew open and in came Steve Fisher, cocky, flash, ebullient, so up himself he wished he was someone else so he could write himself a love letter.

"You'll never guess who I've just played golf with!" he exclaimed excitedly.

Oh, God – I knew *immediately* I was in for a bombardment of narcissistic gobbledygook. He answered before I had time to respond.

"Tiger Woods! Straight up, Tiger fucking Woods! I'm in the shop buying a new putter 'cause my old one snapped in half, he comes in and asks me if I fancy a round as he's in need of some practice. Next thing I know we're on the fucking first, I bring out my driver and hit the best fucking tee shot I've ever hit in my fucking life, goes for fucking miles, 400 yards at least, smack in the middle of the fucking fairway! The fucker couldn't believe his eyes! He literally turned pale! It took him two shots to even get close! Then I get my sand-wedge and chip it straight into the hole. Straight into the fucking hole! A triple fucking albatross! Can you believe that?!"

"Not really, Steve, no."

"True as I'm standing here!"

"There's no such thing as a triple albatross," I pointed out.

"Sure there is! Two shots on a par 5 plus my handicap .... a triple albatross!"

It was pointless arguing. If someone had been to the moon, Steve had been there twice.

"And what exactly was Tiger Woods doing in St George's Hills?" I asked him dubiously.

"I don't know, do I?" he snapped. "I didn't ask!"

He actually seemed to believe it himself. Either he'd dreamt it or there was some guy going round Surrey pretending to be Tiger Woods. Either way, you could be sure that Steve would retell it until reality had been changed through repetition. At last, he actually turned his attention to me and my accident.

"So what's wrong with you, then?"

I stared at him, incredulous.

"Well .... let me see now .... I've got two broken legs, my car's a write-off, and my wife's left me. Apart from that, I'm fine. Absolutely tickety-boo! Thanks for asking."

At which point Nurse Kimberly entered, pleasant and smiling as always.

"Sorry to interrupt, poppet. Have you had a chance to look at the dinner menu yet?"

I knew I had to be quick. Steve's eyes lit up the minute she came in. I had to decide fast or he'd start chatting her up.

"Yes, yes, I've looked at it ...." I said, grabbing it.

"Do you know what you'd like?"

"I know what *I'd* like, darling," he smirked lecherously.

PAINFUL

Oh, no! There wasn't even any preamble. The guy was constantly on heat. I grabbed the menu and studied it double-quick.

"Wild mushrooms on toasted brioche to start .... followed by the cote de boeuf."

"How do you want it?"

"Up the arse 'd be good," he grinned.

I nearly died in my private £150 a night bed.

"Medium rare, please."

"What about desert?"

"I'll have the green tea tiramisu."

"Living the life of fucking Riley in here, en't yer!" he laughed, speaking as loudly as he could to draw Kimberly's attention.

I handed her the menu, relieved she could now leave. But, of course, Steve had to make a lasting impression.

"Can I ask you something, sweetheart?"

"Yes?"

"My mate here .... will he be alright? 'Cause I'm a bit concerned. He won't be a raspberry, will he?"

She looked puzzled.

"Raspberry?"

"Ripple. Raspberry ripple. Cripple."

"Oh! No! Of course not."

"'Cause I'm quite fond of the old tosser, know what I mean? He might be a bit boring and useless, but he's still a human being. And I'd hate to see him end up as a nursing home combo platter, you get my drift?"

Kimberly gave him a small, long-suffering look like she'd heard it all before, then turned and left, closing the door behind her.

"Phor, what a babe! Wouldn't mind having an accident with *her,* know what I mean?"

I couldn't hide my disgust.

"You're pathetic, Steve, do you know that? She's 21 and engaged!"

Steve spread his arms, all innocence.

"I'm not planning to spend the rest of my fucking life with her, am I!"

Then he strolls into the bathroom and starts to have a wee with the door open, something I can't stand! It's so uncouth and unnecessary! Worse still, he started up a conversation while he was doing it.

"So how long will you be in plaster casts for?"

"6 to 8 weeks," I grimaced, listening to the loud noise of his pee.

"You're gonna need a man. A chauffeur-cum-handyman type. Someone to drive you round, do your shopping an' that."

He finished, did his flies up, then re-entered without even washing his hands. I grimaced again. How *did* his wife put up with him?

"I know the very guy! Drove me around for a year when I got banned. In fact, you met him! Scottish guy. Big Al McFadden. Do you remember? He caddied for me once."

Oh, I remembered alright! He reeked of alcohol and fags. Him and Steve shared a bottle of scotch on the way round and they both got so legless they kept falling into the bunkers. We couldn't even finish the game! And his accent was so thick I could hardly understand a word he said.

"Great bloke," Steve continued. "Cheap an' all. Give him a fiver, he's yours for fucking life!"

Don't think so, Steve. Thanks but no thanks. *Definitely* not.

5

Two weeks I was in that room, waiting for my legs to heal sufficiently so I could have plaster casts. It was the most tedious and unproductive two weeks of my life. All I could really do was stare at my feet. True, I had my own telly, but everything somehow reminded me of Yvette – especially *Rip-Off Britain.* I tried to read, but my head was all over the shop.

Toenails. Have you ever stopped to think how extraordinary they are? Extraordinary, that is, in their lack of extraordinariness. I mean, what do they actually *do***,** apart from grow? Mine had always grown at an alarming rate, meaning I had to cut them at least once a week. And here I was, 10-11-12 days after the accident, with these ugly monstrosities emerging like triffids, getting longer by the second. Obviously I couldn't ask the nurses, they had enough on their plate. Also I feel it's a very private thing, like having a number two.

Finally Dr Cox, the orthopaedist not the famous TV scientist, said I was ready for the casts and it was okay to go home as long as there was someone there to look after me. I lied and said there was.

The ambulance guys were brilliant and carried me over the threshold, so to speak. And there I was, back in my delightful little cottage in Weybridge, just me, the walls, the carpets and the furniture, and a hospital full of heartache and grief. I had two legs in plaster, a wheelchair, a pair of crutches, a stairlift that had been installed while I was away, and a whole world of loneliness. I'd been desperate for this day, getting back to my home, being in my own space again, surrounded by my own things. But when I looked around it was meaningless. Totally and tragically meaningless.

I once read a book on Zen, when I was going through my trying to be spiritual phase, that said, *"Loneliness is a power that very few people can handle."* The Zen master was right. And I was one of them. Couldn't handle it at all. Useless at it. Which shocked me because I always thought I could. In fact, I prided myself on it. But when it really came down to it, I needed other people like roses need rain.

Yvette. I missed her noise, her chaos, her knickers and stockings left everywhere. And I started to question why I'd let her go so easily. Maybe I should have fought harder to keep her. But at the same time I knew she was an exotic bird that had to fly. She was too vibrant to remain in one place.

The crutches were pretty useless as both feet needed to be off the ground, so unless you were a Paralympic gold medallist it was easier to use the wheelchair. The trouble with the wheelchair, however, was that it had leg extensions so I could keep both feet elevated, and the trouble with this was that it was virtually impossible to measure the distance between the end of your feet and inanimate objects such as walls, doors and tables, which meant I was forever smacking into them like a clumsy clot, which I found incredibly annoying and also bloody painful!

All I really had to think about was my toenails and how I was going to cut them. Have you ever wondered how to cut your toenails with two broken legs? No, not many people have. But it's a real conundrum, I can tell you! I even asked Dr Cox at one of my follow-up appointments.

"Can't your wife do it?" he said.

"My wife's left."

PAINFUL

"What about your best pal?"

"I don't have one."

"What about the neighbours? Can't you ask one of the neighbours to do it?'

"I can't ask one of the neighbours to cut my toenails! I hardly *know* them!"

He looked stumped.

"Then I suggest you move."

Sometimes I'd get so bored that I'd just ride up and down on the stairlift for hours. Then January 31st arrived. It started raining in the morning and continued throughout the day and into the night. Hard, cold, slashing rain that reflected my mood. And as I sat there in silence with no visitors or phone calls, I realized how insular and isolated my life had become. I felt like an abandoned dog being beaten and kicked. I was fifty-three going on a hundred. It was the most depressing birthday I ever had.

At 7.30 I suddenly found myself searching for the pathetic piece of paper that Steve had given me in the hospital. I discovered it in the washing basket in the breast pocket of my pyjamas. I called. Thirty minutes later the doorbell rang. It was Big Al McFadden.

6

"Hi, Bri, how goes it, ma old mate!"

He wasn't so much 'big' as broad shouldered and hard-looking. And his hands, I noticed them straight away. His hands were *enormous*!

"So you've had a wee accident, eh? Fear not, ma old pal – yer best mucker's here to sort yeez!"

Best mucker? I'd only met him once!

"Shall we have a wee bevvy an' discuss terms, like?"

He was about 5'10", somewhere in his late fifties, but you wouldn't want to pick a fight with him. He had that aura of strength born of confidence and necessity. His life was carved on his features, including several scars and deep lines furrowed around his eyes and on his forehead. They suited him. He was wearing an ex-army combat jacket, skin-tight jeans and trainers, and a t-shirt that read 'I'M GREAT IN BED I CAN SLEEP FOR HOURS'. He was thinning on top and had one of those Mexican-style droopy moustaches.

"I don't do cooking an' I don't do cleaning. I don't do washing an' I don't do ironing ...."

He was knocking back the scotch like there was no tomorrow.

"Mind if I have another one, boss?"

"Sure. Help yourself."

"Cheers, very kinda yeez, don't mind if ah do."

He drained his glass, got up and poured himself one of the largest neat scotches I'd ever seen.

"Nice place, by the way."

"Thank you."

"Must get a wee bit lonely, though, eh? Now that yer wife's left yeez."

"Yes – yes, I suppose so."

Steve Fisher, that wonderfully sensitive gift to the human race, had obviously told him all my private business, the bloody blabbermouth. He probably knew my shoe size and what side I dress on.

"And what do you want me to call you?" I asked.

"Call me anything you like, boss. Most people call me a cunt, but I really dinnae mind."

"How about Al?"

"Sweet."

Then he re-joined me and continued unabated.

"I don't do gardening an' I don't do plumbing ...."

"Perhaps it might be easier .... *Al* .... if you tell me what you *do* do," I intercepted.

"Driving. I don't mind driving. In fact I quite enjoy it. As long as some prick dinnae try to cut us up, in which case I have to get out the motor 'n' punch their fucking lights oot!"

At this point it might be appropriate to mention that I did not approve of Big Al's language and certainly wasn't planning on quoting him verbatim. But to write about him without mentioning the expletives would be like writing about Donald Trump without mentioning the corruption and fake tan. It *was* him, but he somehow made it sound more colourful than offensive, more expressive than threatening.

"Shopping. I don't mind shopping as long as it's Tescos coz the birds are better looking in Tescos, have ye noticed?"

"No – can't say I have," I answered, baffled.

"The ones in Sainsburys are no bad, but the ones in Budgens, by 'n' large, are fucking mingin'! Do you mind if I have a wee smoke?"

"Um .... no .... sure. Go ahead."

And he brings out some rizlas and tobacco and starts to make a rollup. I watched him, trying to ignore the alarm bells in my head.

"And .... how much do you want for driving and a bit of shopping?"

"Och, well, don't wanna be greedy, like – plus we're pals – shall we say, a bullseye?"

"Bullseye?"

"Bullseye a day."

"Sorry .... I don't ...."

"Pinky. Nifty."

"Nifty?"

"Fifty. Fifty a day."

"Ah! Right!"

I noticed he was putting something strange in the rollup, and it suddenly occurred to me that he might actually be making a joint. Now, I've never had one and indeed never seen one being made so I couldn't be sure, but he was certainly adding *something* suspicious!

"But it'll have to be cash coz I don't have a bank account."

"Why not?"

"I don't exist."

I wasn't sure if I'd heard him correctly.

"Sorry?"

"I don't exist."

"What do you mean '*you don't exist*'?"

"I'm wanted by the bacon."

"The bacon?"

"Police."

"What for?"

"I escaped from prison."

I was almost too stunned to respond.

"Barlinnie. Eighteen years ago. Been on the run ever since. So I don't exist. Hope you're ok wi' that, Bri."

PAINFUL

He was so nonchalant about it, it was almost endearing.

"And what were you in for?"

"Armed robbery." He looked at me in all seriousness. "But it weren't me with the shotgun. I want ye to know that, boss. I was only the lookout."

And he lit his rollup and let out an enormous cloud of smoke that almost choked me. I was by now pretty certain it was a joint. For a start it smelt like horse manure and also, immediately, I started to feel light-headed, like I'd had one chenin blanc too many. And for a second, words left my mouth before they'd entered my brain.

"You weren't very good at it, then?"

"Eh?"

"Being a lookout."

"How so?"

"You got caught."

"Aye. I should never 've taken that tab of eckie."

And I found myself starting to find Big Al quite intriguing.

"So what's it like, then .... not existing?"

Then, suddenly, I saw something outside that convinced me I was definitely under the influence of some strange substance. Someone was peering in through the glass. A woman, short, dumpy, absolutely drowning in the brutal, biting rain, wearing only a lightweight summer dress. You could see her underwear through it. A pained expression. I tried not to be too alarmist.

"Um .... excuse me, Al .... but there's a woman staring in through the French windows."

Big Al looked, saw her, and was immediately exasperated.

"Och, for fuck sake!" He turned to me reassuringly. "Don't worry, boss – it's only Morag. I'll sort it for yeez!"

He stood up, marched over to the doors and opened them, livid. She stood there like a pitiful drowned rat.

"What the fuck do *you* want?"

She immediately began wailing.

"Ah had tae see yeez, Ally, ah *had* tae!"

"I told you to wait in the car!"

"But ah'm missing yeez!"

"*Missing me*? I've only bin gone five fucking minutes, ya daft cow!"

"Ya dinnae ken what it's like! Ah cannae bare tae be parted from yeez! Ah *loves* yeez!"

"Well, I dinnae loves *you*!"

She kind of crumpled in a heap.

"No! No!"

"Aye! Aye!"

"But ah'm yer bird! Ah'm yer bird an' yer ma mon! Yeez all ah think aboot!"

"Ma bird? I'd rather shove a monkey wrench up ma arse!" He pointed into the garden. "Now go and stand by that tree. An' don't you *dare* move till I tell yeez!"

"But it's freezing oot here, Ally! Ah'll catch ma death!"

"You shoulda thought o' that before ye interrupted our business meeting! Now fuck off, ya fat slag!"

And he shut the doors again, leaving her to stand in the torrential rain in nothing but her tiny summer dress. He rolled his shoulders and came back in as if nothing had happened.

"Sorry 'bout that, boss."

He sat again.

"Now. Where were we? Och, aye – fifty quid a day an' maybe the odd meal, what d'ya say?"

I literally stared at him in open-mouthed disbelief.

"I'm sorry, Al – but I can't *possibly* employ you *now*!"

He looked mystified.

"How no?"

"You were horrid to her!" I exclaimed. "You just called her a fat slag and threw her out into the rain to die of pneumonia! I can't employ someone who treats women like *that*!"

It seemed to take a moment for it to dawn on him, then he recovered and continued with his usual swagger.

"No, no! You've got it wrong! She *likes* it! She *wants* me to, ya ken?"

I was flummoxed. I'd never heard of anything so preposterous.

"She *wants* you to?"

"Aye. She's sub."

"Sub?"

"Submissive."

"Submissive?'

"She's sub, I'm dom."

"Dom?"

"Dominant."

I still didn't understand. He might as well have been talking Venusian. He read my thoughts and rose again, went back to the French windows, opened them and yelled into the garden where I could see Morag trying to shelter under a tree.

"Morag! Get over here, ya slut!"

She looked afraid and refused to move.

"D'ya hear what I sez? Get yer big fat hairy arse over here NOW!"

"But ye told us not tae move, Ally!" she replied feebly.

"I told you not to move till I *tell* yeez!"
"Aye."
"So I'm *telling* yeez, ya thick tart!"
"But yeez might be testing me! Putting me in a no-win situation!"
"I'll be putting yeez in a fucking boat back to Paisley if you dinnae get over here right this minute!"

She reluctantly left the relative safety of the tree and came slowly, sheepishly back and stood in the open doorway, the rain continuing to pound on her head.

"Tell him!"
"Eh?"
"*Tell* him!"
"Tell him *what*?"
"Tell him you like it!"
"Tell him ah like *what*?"
"Tell him you like me treating ye badly!"
"Ah don't!"
"You do!"
"Ah *don't*!"
"You *do*!"

He looked back at me, almost apologetically.

"She's just saying this to make me look like a twally!"

Then he glared back at Morag, furious.

"You're pathetic, d'ya know that?"

She cowered.

"Ah'm sorry, Ally! Ah dinnae know what yeez want me to say!"

"Nipple clamps for you!"
"No! No!"
"Aye! Aye!"

She suddenly seemed to panic, turned and ran off, yelling as she went. Al started to go after her, then stopped and came back as an afterthought.

"Do you wanna knob it, by the way? It won't mind. It does whatever I tell it!"

By the time I'd worked out what 'knob it' meant, he'd gone and was chasing her round the side of the cottage with Morag screaming hysterically. I dreaded to think what the neighbours were making of it.

I quickly wheeled myself to the French windows and locked them. Then I phoned him on his mobile, told him my legs were hurting and I needed an early night. I heard him drive away and breathed a long sigh of relief. I felt I'd dodged an extremely dodgy bullet.

But that night I couldn't stop thinking about them. Him and Morag. Their lives, they're relationship. What was it actually about? Affection, exhibitionism, some sort of elaborate foreplay? I just couldn't fathom it. And I didn't know why I cared or why it bothered me so much.

I finally fell asleep around midnight with the rain still belting down outside. And that was the end of my 53rd birthday.

7

The next morning the rain had stopped and a strong shaft of sunlight was now hitting my face through the curtains. It was around 9 o' clock and an unusually beautiful Spring-like day. I suddenly heard the landline ringing downstairs, which was unusual. I instinctively pulled back the covers, fell out of bed, and bounced on my bottom to the stairlift in order to answer it in case it was something important.

I got halfway down when it suddenly stopped. I halted the stairlift and sat for a moment, dangling, not sure what to do, whether to continue downstairs or go back to bed. I eventually decided to go back to bed as it had been an extremely restless night. But as soon as I started to ascend, it rang again. I now became determined to answer it and found myself bouncing up and down like a jockey in the Grand National, trying to make it go faster to no avail.

I got to the bottom, leapt onto the wheelchair, and pushed like mad to get to it before it rang off again. I got there and grabbed the receiver, breathless and exhausted.

"Yes? Brian speaking! "

There was a slight pause, followed by a thin, rather tuneless voice on the other end that suddenly started to sing:

"Happy birthday to you
Happy birthday to you
Happy birthday, dear Brian ....
Happy birthday to you!"

"It's not my birthday," I answered flatly.

"What?"

PAINFUL

"My birthday was yesterday."
"Oh."
"What do you want, Yvette?"
"How are you, darling?"
"Me? Oh, I'm fine! Brilliant! Never been better! Yes, yesterday really was a birthday to remember! Rained all day. At one point I think it actually hailed. But it was a marvellous spectacle nonetheless, sitting in my wheelchair, watching it all going on outside. And I even had a visitor! Well, *two* visitors to be precise! A Glaswegian ex-convict who doesn't exist and his girlfriend Morag who likes to be verbally abused. Turned up and performed a sort of human Punch And Judy Show. Very entertaining it was. Then I went to bed, only took me forty minutes to get up the stairs and into my pyjamas, then I closed my eyes and sank into a deep and wonderful sleep, content in the knowledge that being fifty-three, on my own with two broken legs and no friends, really *isn't* all that bad!"

Another pause. She obviously didn't know what the hell I was on about, but I didn't care. I was angry, hurt, disillusioned, and wanted her to know it.

"So what can I do for you?"
"Well ...." she began hesitantly. "I was wondering if you could raise my allowance."

I was dumbstruck. I could hardly believe my ears.

"Your allowance?"
"The three grand you gave me. I was wondering if you could up it to four."
"*Four*?"
"Four grand a month."
"A *month*? No – no, that wasn't three grand a *month*, Yvette! That was a one-off payment to get you out of my hair!"
"*What*?!"

"Four grand a *month*, are you *mad*?!"

"*Three grand*?! You mean that's supposed to last me until I'm back on my feet?!"

"Yes, Yvette! And I think that's very generous under the circumstances, don't you?"

"Well .... no. There's nothing left!"

"You've only been gone three weeks! What the hell have you been spending it on?!"

She immediately went on the attack, like a snake being prodded with a stick.

"It's not easy starting again, you know! I've had to buy a dishwasher, a new toaster, my car's just been in for a service! Plus it's coming up for Valentine's Day!"

"What about Pedro .... or Pablo .... or whatever the hell his silly bloody name is?"

"Paco."

"Paco! Can't *he* support you?"

"He doesn't have your kind of income, darling. He only has three clients and one of them is me. How am I supposed to pay him if you don't raise my allowance?"

It was like trying to deal with the rationale of a two-year-old.

"Give me one good reason, Yvette, why I should subsidize you and your Spanish boyfriend?"

"Because .... because you want me to be happy. Because if I'm not happy I might come back .... but it would be for all the wrong reasons .... and that wouldn't be good for *either* of us."

It was almost admirable. She had the kind of twisted logic that made perfect sense to her but no one else.

"I'll put two grand into your account, but that's it. You'll have to get a job."

"A *job*?"

"Yes – you know – those things people do to earn a living?"

"And what about the divorce? Have you spoken to a lawyer yet?"

I was exasperated.

"I haven't exactly been out and about, Yvette! I'm not especially mobile at the moment!"

"Well, can't *they* come to *you*?"

Thankfully the doorbell rang.

"I have to go."

And I hung up on her, first time ever.

I turned the wheelchair and began the long arduous journey to the front door, past the kitchen, through the dining room, and finally to the porch. In retrospect, I should have got the motorised version, but it was £20 a week more and I wasn't sure how much I'd use it. The doorbell continued to ring persistently as I slowly made my way.

"Yes! Yes! I'm coming!"

At one point they started using the knocker as well.

"Yes! Yes! Alright! I'm going as fast as I can!"

They now rang the doorbell and banged the knocker both at the same time. The noise was deafening!

"What's *wrong* with you?!" I shouted. "You got a doorknocker fetish or something?!"

I finally arrived at the porch, turned the wheelchair to a 45-degree angle, reached up and opened the door, sweaty and dishevelled. I recoiled in shock. It was him – Big Al McFadden – standing there with a big grin.

"Morning, boss! Lovely day! Stopped raining at last, eh?"

And he literally climbed over my protruding legs and entered, totally at home. I turned and followed him, speechless and bewildered.

"Thought I'd get here nice 'n' early, eh? Get a good day's work in, aye?"

He marched into the sitting room with me struggling to keep up.

"First thing we're gonna do is, we're gonna build yeez a ramp. A ramp so you can get in 'n' outa here on the old chariot, like, no bother. Coz you need to get out 'n' about, Bri. Doing yeez no good sitting around here all day getting all mopey, like, getting more 'n' more peely-wally. Gotta get yer life back, boss, eh?"

I tried to intercede.

"Yes .... um ...."

"So we're gonna build yeez a ramp. I've even hired the cement mixer. Coming in an hour."

"Yes .... um .... listen .... Al .... I'm sorry .... but I don't recall actually *hiring* you."

"Eh?"

"Not *specifically*."

He looked surprised, then disappointed, then hurt. I almost felt sorry for him.

"I remember discussing the terms .... but I don't remember actually *agreeing* to them."

He thought for a moment, then recovered.

"Don't worry 'bout it. You don't have to pay me."

"What?"

"I'll do it for nothing."

"*Really?*"

"You're ma buddy, you're ma pal. I'm here for yeez. That's all that matters."

I was humbled and rather moved.

"Oh. Right. Well .... if I don't have to *pay* you ...."

"If you wouldn't mind just reimbursing me for the odd expenses ...."

"Yes. Yes, of course. Least I can do."

"How you off for tools? Hammer, handsaw, drill?"

"Yes, you'll find all that in the garden shed."

"Sweet! Wanna cuppa?"

PAINFUL

And he went into the kitchen and filled the kettle, which felt kind of nice. I couldn't remember the last time someone had made me a brew in the cottage. Certainly not Yvette. It didn't seem to occur to her.

I followed him into the kitchen to show him where everything was but it wasn't necessary. By the time I got there he'd already found the mugs, the sugar and the teabags. Probably the perks of being a bank robber.

"Sorry 'bout Morag last night, by the way."

"Oh .... that's alright."

"She tends to get a wee bit emotional."

"Yes, I noticed."

"She loves me, see. The silly cow's besotted. I keep trying to chuck it but she won't have none. No matter what I do she keeps coming back for more."

I gave a small, friendly laugh.

"Women, eh?"

Then his eyes fell on a photo of Yvette. It wasn't particularly special, it wasn't even framed, just a snapshot of her standing on the seashore in a bikini. I took it myself. I had it there more for the scenery and the memory of a time. The delicious blue sea, the glorious sand, the exquisite palm trees. And Yvette, standing in the middle of it all, hair wet from a swim, looking relaxed and happy.

"Is that her? Is that yer missus?"

"Yes. That's her. Yvette. On our honeymoon in the Seychelles."

"Is that anywhere near Rockley Sands?"

"No – no, I don't think so, Al," I smiled.

He continued to stare at it.

"Fair old body, eh?"

I felt a tinge of pain that Big Al immediately picked up on.

"Sorry, boss! Didn't mean to upset yeez!"

"No. It's fine. You're right – she *has*. Along with other things. That's just a holiday snap. You should see her glossy 10 x 8's. My God, it shouldn't be allowed!"

"Bit of a bummer, eh, her leaving you like that. What with yer accident an' aw."

I felt the hurt again. It shot through me like a flood.

"Yes," I replied quietly. "It hasn't been the best of times."

He regarded me with genuine compassion.

"Never mind, boss. *I'm* here now. We'll soon have you cheered up. Maybe go for a drink at lunchtime, eh, what d'ya think?"

"Sure, why not?"

The kettle boiled and he made the tea.

"Sugar, boss?"

"Just a small amount, please."

He suddenly dipped a tablespoon into the sugar and put an enormous dollop into my tea. He then put three heaped spoonfuls in his own mug, stirring it vigorously. *Three*! Not even teaspoons – *tablespoons*! How he was still alive God only knows! He put the tea in front of us, sat at the table, and began to make a rollup. The tea was the colour of a muddy puddle.

"So how did you get all yer money, Bri?"

I thought I might as well tell him, seeing as how he'd decided to work for me for nothing.

"I'm an angel."

He looked totally blank.

"Lotta money in that, is there?"

"A theatre angel. I invest in shows. Have you heard of a musical called *Phantom Of The Opera*?"

"Can't say I have."

"Andrew Lloyd Webber?"

"Is he that poncey prick what writes all them shite songs?"

"Yes, that's him."

"Posh cunt, aye."

"Well .... when I was eighteen, an aunty left me a thousand pounds and I invested it in *Phantom Of The Opera*. It's been running ever since. And I get a percentage of the box office."

Big Al looked amazed, like it wasn't something normal people did.

"Jeezo!"

"I've invested in other shows since then, of course. The revival of *Oliver* – that ran for four years – nationwide tour of *Billy Elliot* – a play called *The Woman In Black*. Somehow they're always hits."

"And do you get to meet the stars, like?"

"No, I'm just a small investor. But I do get invited to the first night .... and free comps for all the matinees."

"So you just sit here 'n' rake it in, eh?"

"Well, it goes to my accountant *first* .... but yes, I suppose I do. Of course there's always the chance you might invest in a flop, in which case you could lose all your money. Which is why I never invest too much. Just a small amount in case it bombs. A bit like playing percentage golf .... you might not get the eagles but at the same time you won't get the double bogies."

He stared at me, deadly serious.

"You ever lose money, boss, just let us know an' I'll go round there 'n' sort 'em out for yeez. Especially that Andrew Lloyd Webber cunt. I'd *love* to kneecap that prick!"

"I don't think that'll be necessary, Al," I laughed.

But I had a feeling he meant it. He returned to the photograph of Yvette.

"Mind if I take this home wi' me? I don't think it's good for you, seeing her in her wet bikini wi' the see-through bottoms. An' I might wanna look at it when I'm having a poshy."

I had no idea what that was and really had no desire to find out.

I let him take it. The truth was, I had plenty more.

8

Three hours later I was sitting in a very pleasant beer garden somewhere in Hampton Court. It was quite cold but the sun was still shining. There were trees all around, birds were singing, and there was a lovely old couple sipping their half pints of shandy, enjoying their well-earned retirement. It was the first time I'd been out since my accident and it felt wonderfully liberating. Getting there, however, hadn't exactly been smooth sailing.

The cement mixer had been delivered by two rather dodgy-looking men who wanted 'bangers 'n' mash' and wouldn't leave until they had it.

"It's a great deal, boss, coz we get to keep it for as long as we want. They're even throwing in a wheelybarrow and shovel for free. But they want bangers 'n' mash."

"Bangers 'n' mash?"

"Cash."

"No – I'm sorry, Al – I haven't been to a cashpoint recently. Can't think why."

"Ok. Now. I want yeez to trust us here, ok? I'd never do nothing to rip yeez off, you believe that, don't ya? But the guys want bangers 'n' mash an' if I dinnae get 'em it there could be a wee bitta bother, ya ken? So I'm gonna ask ye to trust us wi' your bankcard."

Before I could even answer, he removed his wristwatch and handed it to me.

"Genuine Rolex, worth at least a monkey. It's yours if I don't come back. Ok? Do ye trust us?"

Yes – strangely enough, I did. I honestly felt he was basically an honest person who would never do anything to hurt or fleece me. At the same time, however, I had an uneasy feeling that this whole venture was going to work out rather expensive.

"An' it might be an idea if I get a key cut while I'm there."

I gave him my bankcard, pin number and front door key, and watched him go off in his beaten-up old Ford Sierra while the two men hung around, which I found a bit disconcerting. There was something decidedly unsavoury about them. I kept looking out the window to check on what they were doing. One was sitting in the wheelbarrow, reading a copy of The Sun, the other was pacing up and down like he had somewhere to be.

I dismissed it and went up in the stairlift to get ready for the trip to the pub. I was quite excited. It was the first time I'd been out of my pyjamas and dressing gown. I chose my crewneck fisherman's jumper and tracksuit bottoms which were the only things that went over my plaster casts.

Big Al returned an hour later with the bangers 'n' mash. He paid the blokes who thankfully left, unloaded the bags of sand and cement from his boot, then came inside with all the receipts which reinforced my trust in him. The whole lot came to £125.82p. He'd even itemized everything on a piece of paper in his own spindly handwriting which I found rather charming. He'd been to B 'n' Q because it was cheaper.

Big bagga sand £38
6 bagsa cement £4.02p a bag = £24.12p
Front door key £3.70p
Hire o cement mixer £60
Total amoont £125.82p

PAINFUL

Of course, the front of the cottage now looked like a Wimpey building site. But Al assured me that I'd soon have a super-duper ramp that would give me easy access to the outside world. He decided, however, that it was too late to start work on it now as it was nearly lunchtime and suggested going to the pub instead.

What followed was akin to a roller coaster ride with Charles Manson. Big Al's enormous hands might have been good for terrorizing Morag, but they were virtually useless when it came to manoeuvring a wheelchair. He was completely uncoordinated, he couldn't judge distance, had no spatial awareness, and was totally oblivious to his own strength. From the moment he grabbed the handles and started to push me from the sitting room to the front door, I knew, I just *knew* something bad was about to happen. I even gripped onto the side of the walls to stop him from pushing me any further.

"No. Listen. I'm not sure this is such a good idea, Al. Let's just forget it, okay?"

"Don't worry, boss, I got yeez! I am in complete control!"

He reached over me, yanked open the front door, smacking both my feet, then tipped me so far back I thought I was about to shoot off in Apollo 13. Then I glanced down at the eighteen inches or so drop to the ground and completely lost my bottle.

"No! Please! No!"

But it was too late. He suddenly tipped me totally the other way, promptly depositing me, head first, onto the driveway. I laid there, face down, in complete shock. If I hadn't had a mouthful of gravel I'd have yelled in agony. I heard Al's astonished voice saying something like, "Jesus Christ, how the fuck did *that* happen?!"

Clueless as to what to do next, he stepped over me, carried the wheelchair to the car, folded it and put it in the boot. Then he came back and started to drag me by my plaster casts with me screaming in torment.

"Nearly there, boss, not far now!"

We got to the car and then came the problem of how to get me inside. First he tried to lift me up with the intention of putting me through the sunroof but decided this was too difficult. He then tried sitting in the back and yanking me towards him, but I ended up on his lap. By now I was pleading with him to stop.

"No! Don't! Please, I beg you! I don't want to go! I want to stay here! There's a repeat of *The Gilmore Girls* on this afternoon! Don't make me go, please don't make me go!"

"Don't be so *defeatist*!" he chastised. "We can do this! It's just a case of using our nozzles!"

Finally he turned me around, went to the other side of the car, crawled over the back seat combat-style, grabbed me by my armpits, and pulled me in head first. He then got in the front and we drove off.

The only way I could get comfortable was to stick both my feet out the window, something which proved to be extremely hazardous, especially with motorbikes overtaking at 70 miles an hour. My legs were banging, the end of my nose was throbbing where I'd landed in the gravel, with Big Al just jabbering away like nothing had happened.

"All a question of trial 'n' error, boss. We now know not to stick yer feet through the sunroof coz it's a wee bit uncomfortable for yeez, aye. An' no dropping ye outa the wheelchair coz it's a bit of a pain trying to get yeez back in it again. But now that we've done it once it can only get easier, right? An' once we get a ramp, the sky's the fucking limit! There'll be no fucking stopping us! We'll soon be driving to the Gorbals to meet all ma Scottish relatives, aye!"

I couldn't think of anything more terrifying.

At last, thankfully, we pulled into the pub in Hampton Court, though I did wonder why we'd driven so far for a spot of lunch.

Getting out was a lot easier than getting in, and with the wheelchair placed near to the car door I could almost get in it myself.

While Al was at the bar ordering the food and drinks, I breathed in the fresh air and relished the sun on my face. I'd forgotten how good it felt. And for a moment, just a moment, I forgot all about it – the accident, the broken legs, Yvette and her Spanish boyfriend. Everything leads to somewhere, and maybe this was where I was meant to be. Maybe something amazing was about to happen. Something I could never have foreseen. A bit like Tony in *West Side Story*. Then Al came back with two pints of Fosters.

"There ye go, boss. I've ordered the scampi 'n' chips, should be about ten minutes. Hope you don't mind, but I've left yer card behind the bar in case you want something else."

He sat opposite and we chinked glasses.

"Cheers, Al."

"Lang may yer lum reek!" he declared, and took an enormous swig.

I sipped mine as it was still only one o' clock.

"So tell me about you and Morag," I asked, genuinely curious. "How did you meet?"

He grimaced and shook his head, as though he couldn't believe the terrible fate that had befallen him.

"She answered ma advert," he said miserably.

"Advert?"

"Aye, I advertise in Loot. Personal section."

"*Really*? What does it say?"

He brought out his mobile, found it, and showed it to me. I read it, agog.

'ATTRACTIVE MALE SEEKS ADULT FUN. Assertive male, early 50s, wants to meet broadminded woman married or single for adult fun and games. No objection to middle or upper class ladies applying but must succumb to Scottish manpower. All fantasies fullfiled. BDSM SSC.'

I was speechless.

"What does BDSM stand for?"

"Bondage, discipline, submission and masochism," he answered matter-of-factly.

"And SSC?"

"Safe, sane, consensual."

"And women actually *respond* to that?"

"Aye."

"My God."

"Usually it's a quick in 'n' out job. Short 'n' sweet, like. They come, they go, you give 'em it, they leave. But Morag – Morag came an' never bloody left! She's plagued me ever since!"

"Is that .... is that bad?"

"*Bad*? Have ye seen the fucking state of her? Ted Bundy would 've fucking legged it!"

"Can't you .... can't you just ask her nicely to give you some space?"

He looked at me like I was mad.

"She dinnae ken the concept, boss. She's like a fucking limpet! She's got my number, she knows where I live. If I don't respond she starts stalking me. Straight up, I'm at the end of ma tether! I'm gonna have to do something drastic! Otherwise I'm fucked for life!"

I wasn't sure what to say.

PAINFUL

"You've spelt 'fulfilled' wrong," I mentioned mildly. "It's one 'L' at the beginning and two at the end."

He looked completely disinterested.

I then saw a woman coming towards us. A redhead. Thirtyish. Tall, slim, fair-skinned with freckles, hair in a bouffant, wearing a thin plastic raincoat over bare legs and high heels. She caught my eye and to my surprise came straight up to me and smiled.

"Are you John?" she asked in a thick Brummie accent.

"John?" I replied.

"*I'm* John," Al announced.

"Oh, *you're* John,*"* she said.

"That's Roger," said Al.

"*Roger?*" I queried.

"I'm Marlene," she said.

"Marlene, say hello to Roger," Al ordered.

"Hello, Roger," she obeyed.

"Hello, Marlene," I responded, not knowing what the hell was going on.

"Is Roger going to join us?" Marlene asked John.

"That depends," John answered.

"On what?" asked Marlene.

"On whether he *wants* to," replied John.

"Wants to *what?*" I demanded, suddenly sensing that something strange was happening.

Marlene, quite naturally, now sat and joined us which Big Al seemed to strongly object to.

"Who said you could sit?" he said forcefully, pointing a warning finger at her. "Did I invite you to sit?"

"No."

"No *what?*"

"No, master."

"No, *master*?!" I scoffed, incredulous.

"For that you'll have to be punished. Stand up!"

She stood up.

"Remove yer raincoat!"

She removed her raincoat, dropping it to the ground. Underneath she was naked apart from a tiny pair of knickers. I was in total shock.

"Take your knickers off!"

She took them off.

"Hand 'em to Roger."

She handed them to me. I stared at them in horror.

"What am *I* supposed to do with them?"

"How the fuck should I know!" he snapped at me, as if I was retarded. "Use yer imagination!"

I thought about it, couldn't think of anything, so shoved them in the pocket of my tracksuit bottoms. Marlene was now as naked as the day she was born, apart from her high heels. Al stood up and went to join her on the other side of the table.

"Now bend over!"

She bent over and he began to spank her bottom, hard, again and again. She yelled. The more he spanked her the more she yelled and the more she yelled the louder the yells became, until eventually she was making more noise than Jayne McDonald on a cruise ship. Amazingly, she seemed to really enjoy it. The lovely old couple were frozen in disbelief, their half pints of shandy suspended in mid-air. After a dozen or so slaps, he finished and told her to stand up again. She obeyed. He then brought out a pair of handcuffs, pulled her arms back, and chained her wrists as if she was under arrest.

"*Now* you can sit," he told her bullishly.

She sat, wincing as her backside touched the seat. Then he brought out a leather gag and tied it round her mouth. Marlene was now powerless, unable to move or speak.

PAINFUL

At that point a woman came out holding two plates of food.

"Scampi 'n' chips?"

I self-consciously put my hand up and she placed them down on the table.

"About fucking time!" said Al and sat again, rubbing his hands together and preparing to tuck in.

"Do you have any tartar sauce?" I enquired, trying to contain my embarrassment.

The woman looked at me like there was something wrong with me.

"Who?"

"Tartar sauce."

"Does it come in a sachet?"

"Well .... I don't really know. I've never been here before."

"We only do things what come in a sachet."

"Yes. Fine. Two or three sachets if you've got them."

"You have to get it yourself."

"Sorry?"

"I only bring the food out. You have to get the cutlery and condiments yourself."

I tried to keep my composure.

"You may not have noticed .... but I'm in a wheelchair."

"It *moves,* dunnit?" she remarked indignantly.

Then she suddenly noticed Marlene sitting there, totally naked, bound and gagged. She wasn't quite sure how to respond.

"Does *she* want anything?"

Marlene shook her head. The woman looked blank and went back inside.

"Salt 'n' ketchup," Al complained. "Where's the bloody salt 'n' ketchup?!"

I suddenly lost it and hissed at him through my teeth so that Marlene wouldn't hear.

"What the hell do you think you're playing at?!"

He stared at me innocently.

"How d'ya mean?"

"I thought we were coming for a quiet pint!"

"We *are*!"

I indicated Marlene.

"So what's all *that* about?"

"She answered ma advert. It was arranged before I started working for yeez."

As if that explained everything.

"But why drag *me* along?"

"I thought you'd enjoy it. Bit of an outing, like."

"*A bit of an outing*? Watching someone take their drawers off and get their arse slapped before being bound and gagged? Not exactly a trip to Kew Gardens, is it? And why are you doing it out in the open?"

"She's into E 'n' H."

"What the hell's *that*?"

"Exhibitionism and humiliation."

I leant closer, beside myself with rage.

"I could have been home now .... I could have been home watching Judge Rinder .... or listening to The Archers!"

"But it's not over yet, boss. It gets better. After lunch I'm gonna put a collar on her and take her for a walk!"

9

Just over an hour later there was a complete change of mood, with Al driving, Marlene sitting next to him in the passenger seat, and me in the back still recovering from the sordid, tawdry scene I'd just witnessed.

True to his word, after he'd finished his scampi 'n' chips, he put a dog collar on her with a long chain and took her for a walk round Hampton Court. I don't know if they visited the palace or went in the maze, I didn't ask. I just sat there more miserable and confused than ever. But Marlene seemed as happy as a lark. And Al was suddenly really sweet with her.

"Did you enjoy yerself, hen?"

"Ooh, yes, I had a *lovely* time, thanks very much! And it's really nice of you to drive us home."

"My pleasure," he smiled.

It made no sense. Sitting in the back, with my feet sticking out of the passenger side for fear of motorbikes, I was now able to study her for the first time without the chaos of the initial meeting. She had a nice face, a bubbly personality, a lovely smile and laughing eyes. Ok, she wasn't a film star, but she wasn't unattractive either. Above all, she seemed *decent*. You could imagine her in a nice semi somewhere with a couple of kids and a husband who adored her. So what made her answer Al's advert?

"Where do you live, Roger?" she asked me chirpily.

"Weybridge," I responded.

"Is it posh? I bet it's posh!"

"No, not really. Fairly small, fairly rural part of Weybridge."

"Do you have a maid? I bet you have a maid!"

"No – no maid. I wish I had. I could certainly do with one at the moment."

"And what happened to your legs?"

But before I could answer, this lunatic of a cyclist came racing up on the inside and almost severed my feet off! I yelled, more in shock than anything else.

"These bloody cyclists should be *shot*!" I shrieked. "Think they own the bloody road!"

Al and Marlene seemed alarmed by my outburst, as though it was more surprising than a public spanking in a beer garden completely naked.

We approached a bus stop.

"Drop me off here, would you, John? Don't want the husband seeing us," she giggled.

Al pulled over.

"There you go, darling. Back to sunny suburbia, eh?"

She leaned across and kissed him on the cheek.

"Bye, lover. See you soon."

Then she turned to me with genuine warmth and geniality.

"Ta-ta, Roger. It's been really nice meeting you."

"Nice meeting *you* .... um .... Marlene."

She gave a big friendly smile, then got out the car and went to the bus stop. We both watched as she stood and waited for the next bus that would take her back to normality, whatever that was. Fortunately she'd put her raincoat back on.

"She'll go home happy," remarked Al, satisfied.

As we pulled off, she caught my eye and blew me a kiss. I smiled and waved. As she disappeared from view I seriously wondered what she was going back to – a loving home, gorgeous kids, or a life of banality and boredom.

That night, as I was getting ready for bed, I found her knickers in my tracksuit bottoms. I'd forgotten to give them back to her.

10

The next day I was woken up by the sound of hammering, sawing and swearing.

"Ach, ya cunt yeez! Ya fucking bawsack ye! Ya complete and utter scrotum! Ya useless fucking arsepiece ye!"

Or words to that effect.

I slid from the bed to sit on the radiator to look out of the window to see Al trying to saw a piece of wood, highly harassed, and berating himself as if he was suffering from some sort of duel personality disorder.

"You learnt carpentry in fucking prison, ya cunt! Now you cannae even saw a piece o' fucking wood in a straight line, ya bawbag ye!"

There were bits of wood everywhere. He could have started his own timber yard.

I put on my dressing gown and went downstairs in the stairlift. But when I got to the bottom I realized there was something wrong. No wheelchair. I always left it as close to the stairlift as possible so I could jump straight into it. Suddenly it wasn't there. I sat there dangling for a moment, not sure what to do. I called out, hoping that Al might hear me.

"Al? AL! Hello? Are you there? Al! Come here, I need you!"

The only response was an horrendous scream.

"Ma thumb! Ma thumb! I've smacked ma fucking thumb!"

Suddenly, to my astonishment, Morag appeared in a French maid's outfit, replete with black fishnet stockings, stilettos, one of those tiny white aprons, a little hat, and a dress so short it barely covered her

PAINFUL

behind. She came towards me with a big girly grin, waving a feather duster in the air, full of the joys of spring.

"Mornin', Brian! Did ye sleep well, pet? Yer *must* 've coz yer've had a smashing lie-in, so yeez have! D'ye ken what time it is? It's gone eleven! Ah was starting tae think ah might have tae go up there an' wake yeez!"

"Yes. Um ...."

"Ah've done the hoovering 'n' ah've done the polishing, ah'm just doing a wee bit o' dusting then ah'll start on the windaes."

"Wheelchair."

"Ee?"

"The wheelchair. Where is it?"

"Och, aye. Ah moved it so yeez wouldnae trip over it. Might be a bit disastrous in your condition, eh? Would ye like me tae get it fur yeez, pet?"

"Yes, please."

"Right y'are, darling!"

She threw a big sexy smile, then turned and went into the sitting room while I dangled, bewildered.

She was prettier than I remembered, but that might have been because she no longer looked like a drowned rat. She had a pleasant smile and a bubbly demeanour. And I suppose quite a few men would have found the French maid's outfit quite arousing, even on an overweight forty-year-old of under five foot. Unfortunately, the only one who ever did that sort of thing for me was Yvette. For some reason, she could take me to places a man shouldn't go. Now she was gone – along with my libido.

Morag returned with the wheelchair.

"Would you like me tae pick yeez up and put yeez in it, sweetheart?"

"No thanks, Morag, I can get in it myself."

"Are ye sure? Ah'm a lot stronger than ah look. Ah once won an arm wrestling contest with a bunch o' navvies."

"No, it's fine, *really*. If you could just bring it forward a bit ...."

When I thought it was positioned correctly, I did my usual leap from the stairlift and completely missed the bloody thing, landing on my arse. I screamed with embarrassment, disbelief and pain. Morag gave one of those tiny 'I-told-you-so' tuts, then came round and crouched forward to help me up, her ample bosoms poking out from the top of her low-cut dress. She sounded like a vexed mother.

"Ah've a good mind tae smack yer bottom, Brian, ye stubborn wee bairn, ye! How d'ye expect me tae look after yeez if you dunnae accept ma help? From now on, anything ye need ye ask *me,* ya ken?!"

And she lifted me up and placed me in the wheelchair with the strength of a Sumatran rhinoceros.

"Would ye like a cuppa tea or coffee, darling?"

"Coffee, please."

"Right y'are. Would ye go an' tell Ally ah'm makin' him a tea? He doesnae drink coffee coz it makes him hyper."

And she went into the kitchen, wiggling her bottom flirtatiously as she left. I sat for a moment, trying to imagine Al 'hyper', but it was too staggering a thought to contemplate.

I pushed myself to the front door and looked out. He was now trying to join two planks of wood together with a hammer and nails.

"Ach, ya fucking faggot yeez! Ah TOLD ye not to buy dodgy fucking nails off some cunt on a building site, did ah no? They was BOUND to bend in the fucking middle, ya huddy fucking dobber, ye!"

PAINFUL

Another enormous yell.

"You've smacked yer fucking thumb again, ya fucking twally!"

And this was him *without* a coffee!

"Al? May I have a word, please?"

He saw me and came over, still disgruntled.

"The fucking timber guy, boss, aye! I give him the exact measurements for the joists, what does the cunt do? Measures 'em out in fucking centimetres instead o' feet 'n' inches! I'm having to saw some to make 'em shorter, an' hammer some together to make 'em longer! Apart from that it's going real well!"

"Can you tell me why Morag is in there doing the housework?"

He regarded me curiously, as if I'd asked something glaringly obvious.

"You said you wanted a maid."

"When?"

"Yesterday in the car. Marlene asked you if you had a maid an' you said, 'No, but I wish I did.' So I got yeez one."

"Yes, but .... *Morag*? You said yourself she's emotional. What if she starts flinging plates at you or something?"

"No, no, no! You've got it wrong again! Let me try 'n' explain it to you one more time. She's sub, *right*? She's sub, I'm dom. She don't fling plates at *me* – I fling plates at *her*!"

"But I thought you wanted to get rid of her?"

"I *do*! But your needs come first. An' I might just find a way while she's here to dump the minger once an' for all!"

I still wasn't convinced.

"Well .... how much does she want?"

"Nothing."

70

"*Nothing?*"

"She's doing it coz she likes you."

"*Really*? But she hardly *knows* me."

"Straight up, boss. First thing she says when I dragged her out to the car the other night, '*he seems like such a nice wee man,*' she says."

So it appeared, as luck would have it, I now had a handyman-cum-chauffeur *and* a French maid, both for nothing.

"She's making you a cup of tea, by the way."

Amazingly, he actually paid her a compliment.

"She makes a fine brew. She's fucking shite at everything else – but she *does* make a nice wee brew."

I returned inside and suddenly needed a wee. Must have been all that talk of tea. I went to the stairlift, positioned myself, and did my usual little jump onto the seat. I was just about to pull the lever to go up when Morag suddenly appeared, looking vex again.

"And where d'ya think YOU'RE off tae, mister?"

"Upstairs," I said warily. "I need the loo."

"But ah've jis made yeez a coffee!"

"Which is why I need the loo. You know .... to empty myself .... so I can enjoy it in peace."

"And how long will *that* take?"

"I don't know," I shrugged. "Fifteen minutes?"

"FIFTEEN MINUTES?! It'll be stone cold by then! Why can ye no go doon here?"

"Because the bathroom's upstairs," I replied meekly, once I'd worked out what she was saying.

"Dinnae move!" she ordered, as if I was about to do a runner.

Then she turned and went back into the kitchen while I sat there like an obedient puppy. A moment later she returned with a plastic milk bottle which she tried to hand to me. I stared at it, dumbfounded.

PAINFUL

"You want me to wee into a plastic milk bottle?" I said, incredulous.

"It's nothin' ah havnae seen before," she smiled, somewhat seductively. "Ah used tae work in a care home."

"Well, this *isn't* a care home and I'm not a geriatric .... *just yet,*" I answered, starting to panic.

"Are ye worried about yer aim, pet? Would ye like me tae hold it fur yeez?"

"No!" I shouted, scared.

"Now don't be shy. Ah've done this hundreds o' times!"

And she literally tried to put her hand inside my pyjama bottoms, at which point I noticed Big Al standing there, baring his teeth.

"Leave him alone, ya slut, ye disgusting whore yeez!"

He came thumping towards her.

"I cannae take my eyes off you for five fucking minutes, ya honking spunk-sponge! The minute ma fucking back's turned you're at it, ya stinking faceparty, ye!"

"But ye told me tae be nice tae him, Ally!" she pleaded.

"Aye, I told you to be *nice* to him, I didnae tell yeez to pull his fucking chugger out, did I!" He grabbed her. "Solitary confinement for you!"

"No! No!"

"Aye! Aye!"

And he yanked her back into the kitchen, disappearing from view. I sat, speechless, as the screams began.

"No! Please! Not that, Ally, ah beg yeez!"

"Shut it, ya slagheap!"

More screams. I didn't know whether to go upstairs for a wee or wait to see if he'd murdered her.

Eventually the screams died down and Big Al returned looking rather pleased with himself.

"She won't be bothering you again, boss. I've chained her to the radiator."

My mouth fell open in astonishment.

"You've *what*?!"

"Don't worry – it's her favourite position."

He rolled his shoulders and grinned jovially.

"Now then – I suggest you go up 'n' get ready coz I'm taking yeez out for a truly magical treat!"

I immediately went into a Morag-like panic.

"No! No! Please, Al – not again! Not after yesterday!"

He smiled and shook his head reasonably.

"Naw, that was different! That was all arranged before I started working for yeez. This one's a surprise. A quality surprise .... just for *you*!"

I was immediately suspicious.

"What *kind* of surprise?"

"It wouldn't be a surprise if ah told yeez, would it? Trust me – you'll *love* it! It'll be the best fucking surprise you've ever had!"

"Won't be any more of that S 'n' M stuff, will it?" I asked dubiously.

"Absolutely not!" he answered emphatically. "This is an outing fit for a gentleman! It'll be class, I guarantee it!"

11

An hour or so later we're driving towards the M25 and I'm sitting in the back of the Ford Sierra still doubtful and mistrustful. In fairness, he'd managed to get me out of the cottage and into the car without too much drama. We discovered it was easier to go the back way, through the French windows and around the side of the cottage. It took longer but it felt safer. Then it was just a case of pushing me to the car where I could more or less manoeuvre myself into the back seat unaided.

It wasn't as warm as yesterday and my feet were a bit cold sticking out of the window. I'd chosen the driver's side this time to avoid any more mad cyclists.

It was a nice easy run, with Al seemingly in a calm and relaxed mood after his traumatic experience with the joists.

"So how much did the timber come to?" I enquired casually.

"Just over a nifty. I managed to get 10% knocked off on account he knows me."

"A friend?"

"No, I fucked his wife."

I winced and shook my head in despair.

"And when will it be ready?"

"Eh?"

"The ramp. When will it be finished?"

"Tomorrow. Once I've laid the joists an' I start on the cementing, it'll be a doddle."

"Well, I hope so. It looks like a war zone out there."

"Fear no, big man. I ken exactly what I'm doing!"

We got onto the M25 and started towards Hampshire. We drove and drove and drove. After another hour and something we turned onto the A303 with signs pointing towards The Wallops.

We ended up heading down narrow country lanes with only room for one vehicle.

"Where on earth are we going? We're miles from anywhere!"

"Calmy doony, boss! You'll know soon enough!"

We went through Over Wallop, Middle Wallop, and then Nether Wallop. At one point we had to stop for a cow who was munching on a hedge. Al kept sounding his horn to make it move.

"Fuck off! Fuck off, ya cunt!"

But the cow wouldn't budge, forcing Al to get out the car and start poking it with a stick. He looked scared – Al, that is, not the cow. I let out a yell as another one appeared at the window and started licking my feet.

Another turn into an even more rural backroad where a badger would have had the right of way, and finally, right in the middle of nowhere, we come to a pub – The Dog And Ferret. I couldn't for the life of me work out why we'd driven almost two hours to visit a pub in the middle of nowhere called The Dog And Ferret. But I had a strong sense of foreboding.

We parked virtually outside on a grass verge, I got in the wheelchair, and he pushed me towards the entrance. But just before we went in he told me to close my eyes.

"What for?" I responded grumpily.

"You'll soon find out!" he answered, grinning.

I begrudgingly obeyed.

We entered and he told me to open them again. And there – standing at the bar – someone I instantly recognized and wished I hadn't – Steve Fisher!

PAINFUL

"Hello, Brian, you old fucker!"

Oh, no! My heart sank, along with a few other things. So this was the 'big surprise' – this was what we'd driven halfway across England for – Steve sodding Fisher!

"Raspberry!" he shouted to Al.

"Ripple!" Al shouted back.

"Cripple!" they shouted together and laughed.

"Not looking bad for a raspberry, eh?" Al boasted.

"Taking good care of him, big yin?" Steve observed.

"Aye, he's being treated like a fucking lord!"

"Plenty of girlie mags, eh?"

"Nah, he prefers the real thing!"

"Who fucking doesn't?"

Then Steve turned to me benignly.

"So what'll it be?"

I was so taken aback I didn't answer.

"Oi – raspberry – what do you want to drink?"

I still couldn't quite believe my ears.

"*Me?*"

"Yeah, you. Ain't any other fucking raspberries in here, is there?"

In fact, there wasn't *anyone* in there – apart from two old yokels who were staring at us with suspicion. They obviously didn't welcome strangers in The Wallops.

"*You* want to buy *me* a drink?"

"Don't look so fucking shocked! I'm *always* buying you fucking drinks, yer ponce!"

There are none so deluded as tight-arses.

"I'll have a shandy."

"A fucking shandy? Don't you want something stronger?"

"It's only lunchtime. I don't like drinking at lunchtime."

"As adventurous as ever I see, you miserable old cunt!" He turned back to Al. "What about you, big yin?"

"I'll have a chaser!"

"Good idea! I'll join you!"

As Steve turned round to order the drinks from a miserable-looking landlord who looked as though he wanted to kill us, I took the place in. It was small and drab with nothing warm or comforting about it. No open log fire, no friendly welcoming soul behind the bar. So the question remained – *why*? Why The Dog And Ferret?

Al came down to my level, grinning like a Cheshire cat.

"Howzaboot this, then, boss? Steve fucking Fisher, yer best pal! Laugh a fucking minute wi' that cunt, eh?"

"Oh, *yes*!" I offered sarcastically. "Almost as much fun as my road accident!"

After presumably ordering the drinks, Steve turned back to Al, winking and acting furtive.

"Oi! Ally!"

He closed one nostril with his forefinger, sniffed through the other, then gestured towards the toilets. Al seemed to pick up on it immediately and the two of them disappeared into the gents, leaving me there to ponder my fate. What the hell was I doing here? It was like God wanting to punish me further for a crime I didn't commit.

"Thirteen pound eighty," said the landlord in a broad West Country twang.

Of course! The old Steve Fisher trick of ordering the drinks, then disappearing into the loo when it was time to pay!

"Thirteen pound eighty," he repeated, staring straight at me.

PAINFUL

I reached into my tracksuit bottoms and grudgingly handed him my bankcard. He took it, no change of expression.

"So what brings you fellas to these parts?" he asked as he swiped it.

"I really haven't a clue," I answered wretchedly.

"Crop circles?"

"Sorry?"

"Come for the crop circles, have you? Hundreds round here. All fake, of course. I know the bloke what does 'em – Issy Wickham. Mad as a bleedin' hatter! Goes round on his bike and does 'em with his scythe."

I somewhat doubted Issy Wickham quite had the technology for crop circles, but I didn't say anything. He handed me back my card, at which point the dynamic duo returned. They'd obviously been up to something. Both were grinning from ear to ear.

"Alright, Bri?"

"Ok, boss?"

"That toilet's fucking rank!"

"Aye, I've known cleaner cludgies in the fucking Gorbals!"

And I noticed both had some strange white stuff around their noses and upper lip.

12

An hour later we were sat at a table with both of them completely off their faces, especially Al who kept standing up and making speeches, mostly about me.

"And I'm tellin' ye this! I'm tellin' ye this! This mon here ....this mon here is a *saint*! A fucking saint! He should be fucking consummated! Coz this mon here .... this mon here is the salt o' the fucking earth! An' I'll tell ye something else! If this mon here .... if this mon here cannae make a marriage work .... then NO mon can make a marriage work! Coz this mon here .... this mon here is the finest fucking mon it's ever been ma fucking pleasure tae meet! An' I winnae hear a fucking word against him!"

He downed the rest of his pint, actually managing to stay on his feet.

"Same again, chaps?"

I felt I really had to say something.

"Look .... are you *sure* you're going to be alright to drive, Al? This will be your *third* chaser!"

"I drive better when I'm pished," he slurred.

"Yeah, I can vouch for it," added Steve, desperately trying to focus.

"D'ya think ye could lend us a wee sub, eh, boss? On the old expenses, like, so I can buy yeez all a drink?"

I should have seen this one coming.

"I don't have any cash."

"Tell ye what – why don't I put yer bankcard behind the bar – start a wee tab, like, eh?"

This was the story of my life. People taking advantage and me falling for it. Even my best friend from college diddled me out of fifteen grand. For some reason, I'm not sure why, I always found it difficult to say no.

As I handed him my bankcard a tear came into his eye.

"Yer ma buddy, yer ma pal! An' I'm gonna look after yeez till the day ah fucking die!"

He turned and staggered to the bar. He had trouble finding it. He was all over the place. It was then I realized the full extent of Al's inebriation.

"He's completely *legless*!"

Steve laughed.

"Hark who's talking!"

He burped and downed his scotch. His eyes were glazed, he had an inane grin, and there was more of that white stuff around his nose.

"*And* you!" I said accusingly. "What have the two of you been doing?"

"Doing?"

"You've been in and out of that toilet nonstop!"

He smirked like a simpleton.

"Just .... just a few lines of charlie."

"Charlie?"

"Blow. Snort. Cocaine."

Class A drugs. I should have known. I was livid!

"Right! That's it! I'm going home! I'm calling for a cab and leaving!"

"Leaving? Don't be fucking stupid! A cab from Little Wallop all the way back to .... back to .... wherever that shithole is you come from .... it'll cost a fucking *fortune*!"

"I don't care. I'm bored, okay? I want to go home!"

Then something more important caught his eye.

"Hello, hello, hello! There she blows!"

A woman had appeared behind the bar, wearing a low-cut see-through blouse, bra and cleavage exposed to the max. She had dyed black hair and three weeks' worth of makeup. Getting on a bit, to say the least. Brash, vulgar, tarty, mutton dressed as lamb. And I knew, I knew *immediately,* that this was why we'd come to The Dog And Ferret.

Steve got up and swayed to the bar to have a word with Al who was still getting served by the miserable-looking landlord. A quick exchange, then Steve continued to the other end of the bar to have a word with the mutton dressed as lamb. Then Al came back with all the drinks half-spilt on a tray. He sat down to speak to me with drunken discretion.

"So what I'm thinking, boss, is .... maybe it might be a good idea to stay the night."

I stared at him in horror.

"*Stay* the night?"

"Apparently they got rooms at extremely competitive rates."

"*Stay the night?*! Are you *mad*? I can't think of anything worse!"

"Well, it's either that or spend the night in the Ford Sierra. Coz to be quite frank .... the only way I'm not passing out is if I keep drinking."

I was angry.

"This is *outrageous*! This is unacceptable! This was supposed to be for *me* – 'an outing with class' you said!"

"Aye, it *is!*"

"This is no more for me than it is for Children In Need!" I sneered. "This is for *you* – you and that debauched sex-addict cohort of yours!"

"*An'* you."

"*Me?*"

"Steve an' I have discussed it .... an' we both feel that what you need is a damn good knobbin'."

PAINFUL

My mouth recoiled in disgust.

"With *her*?"

"Aye. Bangs like a door in a gale. An' best of all .... Steve reckons she'll go with *anything*. Which is great news for you!"

I took another look, appalled. The *most* you could say about her, without being disrespectful, was that she looked okay from a very long distance.

Steve now returned looking like he'd accomplished vital trade talks with China.

"Right. All sorted. She'll take us *all* on – even Brian. She was a bit reluctant at first, but I talked her into it. Along with fifty quid, of course."

"No. No way. Absolutely not!"

"Why not?" asked Steve, bewildered.

"*Why not*? She's got to be at *least* sixty!"

"Nah!" he reasoned. "Fifty-eight, fifty-nine at the *most*! And I reckon she's in pretty good nick for her age! I mean, she *smells* alright. Plus she's got a fair pair o' pins – once you get over the varicose veins."

"No. No thanks. Very kind of you – but definitely *not*."

"Stop being so fucking fussy! How long's it been, eh? How long's it been since you dunked yer dick? One month, two months? And there it is – all set up and waiting for you on a plate!"

"And how am I supposed to do it with both my legs in plaster?"

Steve thought about it.

"We'll wheel you in."

"No, it's alright, thanks. I'd rather remain celibate, if it's all the same to you."

"Suit yourself, you miserable old cunt. Try an' do you a good turn and this is what we get!"

"*I* think she's a highly attractive woman," slurred Al through extremely dodgy beer-goggles. "What's her name again?"

"Doris."

"Nice name."

"Aye, big yin. And you've never had a ride like it. The woman's *insatiable*!"

"What's that mean?"

"Can't get enough, yer div!"

"Can I dominate her?"

"You can tie her up and set light to her clit for all I care!"

"What about her old man? Where will *he* be?" Al asked, indicating the landlord.

"Don't worry about him. They don't speak. They hate each other. She sleeps upstairs, he stays in a caravan out the back."

"That's good. Coz I'd hate him to hear me sausaging her up."

I honestly felt like I'd died and gone to Butlins.

"My God," I scowled. "Could you two sink any lower?"

"Aye – *I* could," Al said proudly.

"Have you no shame?"

"No," Steve answered matter-of-factly.

"What about your wife?"

"She's got thrush. I ain't had nothing for a week. I'm fucking *desperate*!"

His attention suddenly went to his drink, most of which lay swimming in the rim of the tray.

"What's happened to these fucking drinks, Al? There's more in the fucking tray than there is in the glass! You in need of a guide dog 'n' stick or something?"

PAINFUL

He downed the scotch in one, then stood up, irritated, and disappeared back to the bar for a refill.

Al and I now sat in stony silence. I was too annoyed to speak. Al suddenly looked ashamed. Then, to my surprise, he started to cry. Literally. Held his head in his hands and sobbed like a baby.

"I'm sorry, boss! I didnae mean to get into this state! Forcing ye to stay the night an' aw. Ah feel real bad about it. Real fucking bad! I feel so fucking bad I could murder myself!"

I regarded him with scepticism.

"Do you think you could wait until after you've finished the ramp, please? My property's devalued by thousands since you started on the bloody thing!"

And on and on it went, hour after hour, drink after drink. And more visits to the loo. There wasn't even any food. The 'chef' was off with food poisoning, presumably after eating their own cooking. I had a bag of crisps and some pork scratchings. The other two didn't seem particularly hungry. They'd just go back to the toilet for some more 'charlie'.

By eight o' clock I decided to go to bed. This, of course, turned out to be one of the most dangerous and truly torturous experiences of my life. There was no lift, so I had to be pushed up a steep and narrow staircase that felt like ascending Kilimanjaro. And who did I have behind me? A drunken, coked-up Scottish lunatic who kept assuring me it would be fine.

"Don't worry, boss, I got yeez!" Then in the next breath, "Oh fuck, I'm going! I'm fucking going! I cannae hold yeez! We're slipping! We're fucking slipping!"

Steve, of course, had declined to help on account of his bad back which he'd never mentioned in all the years I'd been playing golf with him.

"Ma arms! I cannae feel ma arms! I cannae breathe! We're gonna fall! Any minute now! We're gonna fucking fall!"

Thirty minutes it took! Thirty long minutes! I kept imagining both of us plummeting to our deaths and ending up as a documentary on Netflix.

We finally made it. It was like surviving the electric chair only to discover you were now being sent to Guantanamo. We found the 'guest room', which was as inviting as a cold shower. To call it basic would have been an understatement. A wardrobe, a sink, a double bed and a tiny cot-bed in case some hopeless parent actually decided to bring their three-year-old on a jolly jaunt to The Dog And Ferret. Drab patterned wallpaper, threadbare rug, and a smell of damp. Al swayed from side to side, desperately trying to stay upright.

"What a magic room, eh, boss? D'ya want the double bed .... to share wi' me, like? I havenae cut ma toenails for a wee while, but I had a bath about a week ago so ah should still smell fairly fresh."

But I was not ready for forgiveness.

"No. I'm sorry, Al, I'm fuming, I really am! I'm not happy about this, I'm not happy about this *at all*!"

He looked mortified, then immediately began to cry again.

"Oh, Jesus! You're scunnered! I've scunnered yeez! Oh, Jeezo! I'd rather have got ma bawsack chewed by a chihuahua than have ye scunnered wi' me, boss!"

"Oh, shut up," I said dismissively. "Go back to your junkie pal, have some more cocaine, and leave me in peace!"

I couldn't even be bothered to get undressed. I fell fully clothed into the cot-bed, both plaster casts sticking out the end, and determined that Big Al McFadden would have to go.

13

It was difficult to get to sleep. I felt like I'd been mummified. But I eventually managed it, even with all the laughing and shouting still going on in the bar downstairs which was clearly audible.

An indeterminate time later I was suddenly awoke by Steve and Al coming into the room, clumping and staggering, making no effort whatsoever to keep the noise down. Steve saw me and laughed.

"Get fucking Goldilocks sleeping in Baby Bear's bed!" he roared.

I kept my eyes shut and pretended to be asleep so I wouldn't have to engage. Then there was a massive clump when one of them, I think it was Al, walked straight into the wardrobe. They were obviously too drunk to feel it.

"Soo .... er ...." Al began, desperately trying to string two words together. "How we gonna do this?"

It seemed to take Steve ages to figure out what he was on about.

"What do you mean?"

"How we gonna .... ya know .... *do* it, like?"

"Do *what,* yer cunt?"

"Go in, like? I mean .... do we go in together .... or do we go in separate?"

Another long gap while Steve processed this conundrum.

"You wanna watch me knob her?"

Another long gap while Al thought about it.

"Not *especially*."

"Right, then. We go in separate."

PAINFUL

But Al still remained perplexed.

"An' does she know we're different guys? Or do we pretend to be the *same* guy?"

Steve now sounded totally confused.

"It don't matter! Who gives a shit? If *she* don't mind, why should *we*?"

"An' do I go in as you're coming out .... or do you come out as I'm going in?"

"Eh?"

"Or do I go out as *you're* coming in?"

"You know what, Al? You talk complete and utter shite, son. Straight up, you're like a fucking foreign film with dodgy subtitles!"

"Just trying to get it straight, Steve."

"I go in .... then *you* go in."

"You go in .... then *I* go in."

"Yeah. *I* go in .... then *you* go in."

"So .... you go in first, like."

"Unless *you* wanna go in first. Do *you* wanna go in first?"

"Aye – well – *maybe*. I mean .... it's a tough decision. Coz, like .... if *I* go in first she'll be nice 'n' fresh .... but if *you* go in first she'll be nicely warmed up."

"'Ere, Al – show me that picture of Brian's missus again – get me in the mood."

Al found the photograph I'd given him of Yvette and handed it to Steve. I remained motionless, still pretending to be asleep, listening to one of the most openly misogynistic conversations I'd ever heard.

"Phor, look at that! You can see her fucking nipples!"

"Aye, she's just back from a swim."

"Looks a right dirty cow!"

"Great bangers."

"Bet she takes it up the arse, no bother."

"Used to be a model."

"Which leaves the question .... what the fuck was she doing with a boring old fart like Brian?"

"Maybe he's got a massive Bobby Dangler."

"Yeah, and maybe she's got a massive nose for a healthy bank account!"

"Aye, he gets paid by that Andrew Lloyd Webber cunt."

"Tell you what, Al – *you* go in first. I'm gonna stay and have a wank."

And that's when I lost it. Totally, completely and irrevocably. I sat up and threw the pillow at them, beside myself with rage. It hit Al in the head and he froze in shock. Steve just stood there, still clutching the photograph, trying not to laugh.

"WILL YOU TWO SHUT UP! SHUT UP! JUST SHUT UP! I've had enough! I can't take any more! You're *disgusting*! *Both* of you! You're animals! You're depraved! You should both be *castrated*! Yes, that would put an end to your sordid, twisted games, WOULDN'T IT! And what about *me,* eh? What about ME?! This has been the worst day of my life! I've got two broken legs, I'm supposed to be *convalescing*! And what do *you* two do? Bring me to the pub from hell! Cold, smelly, nothing to eat! A landlord that looks like he wants to slit my throat! And all I've heard all day is you two banging on about raspberry ripples and how I need a damn good knobbing! And *now* you're even defiling a photograph of my wife! WHAT'S WRONG WITH YOU?! Can't you think of anything else?! You're *obsessed*! And as for *her* .... the landlord's missus .... she's ready for the knacker's yard! She should be tucked-up in bed with a nice hot water bottle and a cup of cocoa! If she was any older she'd be getting a telegram from the Queen! What about sexually transmitted diseases, eh? Have you thought

PAINFUL

about THEM?! You could pass them onto your loved ones, you fools, you idiots! Have you no morality or guilt? No, of *course* not! Because you're not capable of it! You're too damned selfish! All you think about is *you*! You and that insatiable lump of throbbing gristle between your legs! Well, I've had it! I've had it with *BOTH* of you! I just want to get through tonight, survive this horrendous ordeal, go back to my boring life in Weybridge, and forget I ever met you! You're two of the most selfish, disgusting, despicable degenerates it's ever been my misfortune to know! And I never, EVER want to see either of you ever again! Do you hear me? EVER AGAIN!"

That was it. I was finished. I had no more energy. I fell back, panting with the passion of my outburst. They both stood there, Al speechless, Steve defiant.

"What's up, Goldilocks, got your period?" he grinned facetiously.

14

It was a long, slow, excruciating night. First Al went in – then Steve went in – then Al went in again for a return bout. Bedposts banging, floorboards pounding, yells and screams. It sounded like a scene from *The Exorcist.*

And having them in the same bed next to me was not a pleasant experience. Al kept snoring and passing wind in his sleep, Steve kept kicking him and calling him a "noisy fucker" before getting up to have another wee in the sink. He must have gone at least a dozen times, his bladder obviously as overactive as his mouth. The bed groaned and creaked every time one of them moved.

The next morning was gruesome. No toothbrushes or toothpaste, of course. The bathroom was the other end of the hall with no clean towels, we'd all slept in our clothes and looked and smelt terrible, apart from Al who roughly smelt the same.

Then came the daunting task of getting me down the stairs. Getting *up* them had been bad enough, but going *down* them felt even more death-defying, with Al sweating and shaking from a hangover and me grabbing onto the sides of the stairwell petrified. I looked down and all I saw was a sheer drop to oblivion. I completely froze.

"No. Forget it. I'm not going."
"Eh?"
"I'm not going! I'm staying here!"
"Staying *here*?"
"I'm *not* going down those stairs!"
"But .... how ye gonna eat?"

PAINFUL

"Go and get some help."

"Eh?"

"HELP! Get some help!"

He glanced around, befuddled.

"There ain't no one, boss. Steve's in the bathroom having another wank."

"Not *Steve*! *Anyone* but Steve! Someone else! I'm not dying in this way, being pushed down a flight of stairs by an inebriated nutter with no coordination!"

"Who's that, then?"

"Just go and get some help – *now*!"

Still looking confused, he left me at the top of the stairs and went down to find someone.

Twenty minutes later two butch-looking firemen suddenly appeared from nowhere and came running up the stairs with pickaxes. The idiot had rung the fire brigade. One of them threw me across his shoulder and carried me down in a fireman's lift while the other brought the wheelchair.

I paid the bill. It came to £420. The room alone was £180, and all the drinks came to a whopping £240, including a dozen 'kamikazes', whatever the hell they were, at a fiver each. I'd been fleeced. I was furious. Al sensed my displeasure.

"Did it come to a lot, boss?" he cringed.

I glared at him angrily.

"Yes, you might say that!"

"You'll get it back. Every penny, I swear it. Tell ye what – I'll work for yeez for nothing, how's that?"

"You *already* work for me for nothing, Al. Hardly the deal of the century, *is* it?"

As we came out of The Dog And Ferret, Steve appeared with his usual cocksure arrogance and Essex-boy strut.

"See you around, raspberry."

"Not if I see you first," I snapped.

He stopped and smirked.

"You really are an uptight cunt, Brian, you know that? You need to chill-out, son."

I regarded him with undisguised disdain.

"Why don't you go home to your wife, Steve? Why don't you try being faithful for a change?"

"Faithful like you, you mean?"

It hurt. It struck a nerve, but I pretended it didn't.

"Yes – faithful like me."

Another grin. Then he swaggered to his brand new F-Type Jag convertible parked just up the road. Al unlocked the back door of the Sierra and I pulled myself in. We drove off in silence.

As we left the quaint rural charms of Little Wallop and got back onto the open road, Al asked me the most ridiculous question I'd ever heard.

"Did ye have a good time, boss?"

I was too flabbergasted to answer. Then he noticed something in his rear-view mirror.

"Oh, shite! It's the bacon!"

He suddenly changed gear and slammed his foot on the accelerator. Abruptly a police siren started up, we're going 80 miles an hour in his rickety clapped-out old motor, and I'm being tossed around like a gerbil in a spin dryer.

"Hang on, boss! I think we're being followed!"

And now we're in a car chase that wouldn't have come amiss in an episode of The Sweeney. Screeches of tyres and brakes as we overtake and weave in and out of the traffic, angry drivers sounding their horns, and another car crash, the second in five weeks, loomed large. I cried out in desperation.

"For God's sake, Al, give yourself up! It's not worth it! Prison can't be *that* bad surely!"

PAINFUL

I felt a sharp turn and we suddenly slammed to a halt. The police car went by and the siren gradually faded. A short, mystified silence.

"Jeezo, that was close! Ah thought I was going back to fucking Barlinnie for a minute! Obviously on their way to an accident. Good job it weren't *us,* eh?" he laughed hysterically.

I clenched my teeth, unable to find the right expletives.

15

He pushed me to the front door and opened it with his key. He got me past the porch then looked at me with that pitiful hangdog expression that he used every time he was in trouble.

"Do ye still not want to see us again?" he asked forlornly.

"Yes, Al – you are correct – I *really* don't want to see you again. It's been a blast, it really has – and I wish you every success in the future – but please, please, PLEASE – go and work for nothing for someone else. Because so far it's cost me an absolute arm and a leg and been about as much fun as a night out with Hannibal Lecter!"

By his expression, he wasn't sure if that was good or bad.

"What about the ramp?"

"I'll get a reputable firm to do it – it might be slightly quicker and cheaper. Goodbye, Al."

I turned the wheelchair to go inside.

"Boss ...."

I reluctantly turned back.

"Your key."

He handed it to me with all the gravity of a Shakespearean actor. It was like the end of a marriage. I took it and closed the door. I heard him drive away. I went into the sitting room and it immediately hit me – I was alone again. It struck me like a thunderbolt. Emptiness, silence. No one there. No one to talk to. No one to eat with. And it scared me. And I started to look for answers. Maybe it was *me*. Maybe I was too stiff, too rigid. Played it too straight, like my golf.

PAINFUL

Loneliness is different from solitude. Solitude is something you choose – loneliness is forced upon you. Wise men seek solitude, only fools seek loneliness. Solitude breeds knowledge, loneliness crushes it. And though I'd chosen this, it didn't feel like I was on the crest of some amazing self-discovery. I was simply back to square one. It felt cold and harsh and unnecessary.

Suddenly from the kitchen I heard a small frail voice feebly calling out.
"Brian .... Brian .... is that you?"
It took me a moment to process it, then I went in and there she was – on all fours with her bottom in the air – Morag, still attached to the radiator by a metal chain wrapped around her wrists and any escape made impossible by a padlock. She was distressed and dishevelled, her French maid's outfit now looking crumpled and sorry for itself.
"Can you get Ally tae unlock us, please, Brian?" she asked pathetically. "Ah'm dying for a wee!"
She'd been there almost twenty-four hours. She'd had nothing to eat apart from some corn flakes that he'd left for her in a bowl on the floor. She must have been frying alive when the heating was on and freezing to death when it wasn't.
I phoned him. He came back. Of course he'd lost the key. He got a hacksaw from the shed and began sawing, with Morag becoming more and more hysterical.
"You're gonna saw ma hand off, Ally!"
"Shut up, ya slut! An' stop moving!"
"Ah cannae help it! Ah'm desperate for the loo!"
"You'll be desperate for a new head in a minute!"
It was outrageous. It was insensitive and cruel. And yet .... Morag would forgive him. Not only forgive him

but continue to love him and stand by him no matter what. And I started to think .... who was better off? Them or me?

PAINFUL

PART TWO

In At The Deep End

PAINFUL

16

The Skin Club was a little-known underground dive somewhere in Soho that Big Al frequented regularly. Most of the time it was a gay club called *Stallions*, but once a month it became The Skin Club and a night of bondage, whips and sadomasochism. It wasn't advertised so the only way you'd know about it was word of mouth. There was no membership but you had to adhere to a strict dress code – rubber, leather or PVC. To that end, Al turned up with several items of clothing for me. A black PVC waistcoat, a biker's hat, and a real leather gladiator kilt that wouldn't interfere with my plaster casts.

"I feel a bit of a dick in this get-up, Al, I don't mind admitting."

"Naw, ye look *great,* boss! Dead sexy! You'll pull no bother, trust us!"

He was wearing a skin-tight pair of latex trousers, biker boots, and a biker hat that matched my own. He also insisted on both of us going bare chested as it would attract more attention. I reluctantly went along with it even though I felt extremely self-conscious. It was also bloody cold!

He pushed me into a small, dimly-lit corridor. At the end was a girl behind a table wearing the tightest dress I'd ever seen. How she got into it was a mystery. Not only that – her breasts were hanging out!

"It's a latex underbust spanking dress," Al informed me knowingly, as if reading my thoughts.

It was forty pound to get in. I paid with my trusty bankcard which, with amazing foresight, I'd tucked inside my jockey y-fronts underneath my gladiator kilt.

PAINFUL

The girl stood up, followed by her breasts, and stamped our hands with a skull and crossbones in florescent ink.

To our right was a door that looked like the entrance to a dungeon. You could hear loud heavy music pounding from inside. We were about to go in when Al came round to speak to me with a serious and solemn expression.

"Ok .... listen .... this is dead important. What are you?"

I wasn't sure.

"Cold," I answered.

"No, what d'ya fancy?"

"A diet coke."

He looked slightly impatient.

"Are you sub or dom?"

"Oh. Um. I'm not sure."

"You've *gotta* be sure!"

"Why? Can't I decide when I'm in there?"

"No! You have to decide *now*! D'ye wanna give or receive?"

To be honest, I wasn't planning on doing either. In fact I wasn't even sure why I was there. I'd had a conversation with him about how I wanted my life to change, how I was fed up with waiting for something extraordinary to happen, and this was what he came up with.

"Receive, I suppose," I shrugged.

"Right! You're sub. And yer gonna need a safe word."

"Safe word?"

"In case you want 'em to stop."

"Stop *what*?"

He looked at me like I was a lost cause.

"Whatever it is they're doing when you want 'em to stop!"

I nodded without a clue what he was on about.

"Raspberry," he announced.

"Sorry?"

"Raspberry. That's yer safe word – raspberry."

"Why?"

"*Why*? Coz you'll remember it! *Raspberry.* Raspberry ripple. Cripple."

"Well, which one *is* it?"

"*Raspberry!*"

"Right."

"One more thing. When they play *Bolero* .... you scarper."

I stared at him mystified.

"When they play *Bolero* I scarper."

"Aye. Coz that's when all the heavies come out. An' ye don't wanna be messing wi' the heavies!" he warned.

We entered a bizarre, fascinating, mind-boggling world of exhibitionism and eccentricity. A parallel universe of nipple clamps, men in leather thongs with chains around their necks, being yanked by vamp-like creatures in rubber underwear brandishing whips. Crutchless G-strings, cat masks, basques and corsets. Adult schoolgirls in stockings and suspenders. I stared around in wonderment and awe as Al parked me to the side of the dance floor and went to the bar to get some drinks. Even more amazing, he said he was buying as he'd had a win on the horses. To celebrate I changed mine from a diet coke to a red wine.

The dance floor was packed, mainly with women – although there were a couple of men pretending to be women – and a couple of women pretending to be men. Or maybe they were *all* pretending. Who the hell knew or cared?

I suddenly became aware of a tall, unbelievably thin man standing next to me in nothing but a leather codpiece and a dog collar. He was completely bald and scarily pale. He looked like he'd just risen from the dead.

"Hello. My name's Keith. What's yours?"

"Roger," I responded.

"I'm into CBT."

"Jolly good," I smiled.

"What about you?"

"No, I prefer Classic FM."

I later found out that CBT stands for 'cock and ball torture'. Thank God I assumed it was a radio station!

Keith left, only to be replaced by a short, stubby man in a bonnet and rubber diapers, holding a large baby's bottle. He was about five foot with the smoothest skin I'd ever seen.

"I've done poo-poo!"

"Oh dear," I grimaced.

"Daddy change me?" he asked optimistically.

I was immediately filled with fear and dread, followed by one of the strangest conversations I'd ever had.

"No. Sorry. I'm not equipped."

"But baby got squeaky bottom."

"Where's mummy? Go and ask mummy."

"Mummy being whipped by naughty vicar."

"Well, ask one of the women with their breasts out. There's plenty to choose from. It probably means they're mumsy."

Suddenly I got pushed from behind onto the dance floor. I assumed it was Al having a laugh, but when they swivelled me round I saw it was a young sexy nurse in an all-white uniform, with white stockings and suspenders to match. She was gyrating energetically to some modern-day tune where they talk instead of sing.

It seemed she wanted me to participate, though quite what she expected me to do in a wheelchair God only knows. I tried to indicate the man in the baby's diapers as I thought they'd be better suited. She totally ignored me, cocked her leg over my plaster casts, and started rubbing herself against them. It hurt like hell! I screamed for her to stop but the silly cow persisted, oblivious. The pain was intense! Only one thought entered my head – where the hell was Al? He'd been ages!

All of a sudden the lighting changed and the music became a slow, sensuous, almost hypnotic rumba-like instrumental that I immediately recognized but couldn't place. Straight away the nurse stopped gyrating and dismantled. The dance floor cleared. I watched them retreat, puzzled and fascinated. They now stood around the edges of the dance floor, forming a voyeuristic circle. I couldn't work out what was going on. In their place emerged three or four extremely weird-looking people holding bull-whips and various instruments of torture. They circled around, staring at the crowd, inviting people to step forward. Among them was this 'thing' the likes of which I'd never seen before. It pertained to be a woman but was well over six feet with broad masculine shoulders, wrestler-like arms, and legs like tree-trunks. It was squeezed into a small red PVC dress with a split right up the middle to the crutch where its genitalia was on full display. I didn't look so therefore remained in the dark as to what it was. It was wearing thick, scary, vamp-like makeup with peroxide-blonde hair scraped back into a ponytail. It was also wearing bright red platform boots to match the dress, making it even taller. It had a fierce expression and was brandishing a cane. The overall effect was *horrific*!

Its eyes suddenly settled on me. It came up and glowered down at me.

"So you wanna party, do you?" it said in a deep, formidable voice.

I stared back and trembled.

"Sorry? No! No! Absolutely not! I didn't realize ...."

"SHUT UP!" it shouted, and suddenly brought the cane down on the side of the wheelchair with an enormous THWACK!

"You don't speak! You don't speak unless *I* say you can! Understand?"

I didn't answer. I wasn't sure if I was allowed.

"*Understand*?!"

He/she/it brought the cane down again, another enormous THWACK! I still didn't answer. I was frozen in fear and uncertainty. It now brought the cane down five more times, emphasizing each syllable.

"DO .... YOU .... UN ....DER ....STAND!!!"

I screamed and cried out in desperation.

"Yes! No! I'm not sure! Can I speak or *can't* I?"

It clenched its teeth and snarled menacingly in my face.

"You know what you are, don't you?"

I shook my head in dread.

"An invalid?"

"A naughty, disobedient little boy! And you know what we do to naughty, disobedient little boys, don't you?"

"Not really," I whimpered.

"We .... *thrash* them!"

I instinctively covered my head with my hands.

"No! Don't! Please! I beg you! I'm new at this!"

But the monstrous creature, who quite frankly made Godzilla look sweet, completely ignored me and started whacking away like a thing demented.

"Don't mess with me, sonny! I'm the real thing! You wanna play with me, you better be prepared for *pain*!"

I screamed and writhed to avoid the blows.

"No! No!"

"I'm a *professional*! I don't piss about!"

"But I don't like it! It hurts! I want to go home!"

Then I suddenly remembered what Al had said about a 'safe word' to get them to stop. But I couldn't remember it. I knew it was some kind of fruit, but I was too flustered to recall it.

"Orange! Pineapple! Melon!"

More whacks.

"Banana! Mango! Seedless grape!"

Then it suddenly came to me.

"RASPBERRY! Yes, that's it – RASPBERRY!"

It stopped thrashing for a moment and stared at me like I was mental.

"What do you mean?"

"RASPBERRY! RASPBERRY!" I pleaded, near-hysterical.

But the thing bared its teeth and became even more aggressive.

"Who you calling a raspberry, you pathetic little faggot!"

And that's when it *really* started lashing out with uncontrolled frenzy like a beast unleashed. Fortunately most of the blows landed on my arms and shoulders, but it was still a terrifying experience with no end in sight. Then a miracle happened – Keith, the man in the leather codpiece, stepped forward.

"Me! Me! Let it be me, oh divine mistress of cruelty!"

It grabbed him by his dog collar and yanked him closer.

"You want it hard or soft?"

"Hard! Hard!"

PAINFUL

"Ok, sonny – you want it, you got it!"

And it flung him to the ground and began hitting him right on the money. Keith writhed and squealed in agony, but you could tell he was loving it. Then Al appeared and took charge of the wheelchair, hurriedly pushing me away from the crowd to another room off the dance floor. A makeshift sign above the door read 'The Love Room'.

It had soft pink lighting with foam rubber flooring and offered relative calm and safety from the rest of the club. The volume of the music also decreased considerably. I didn't really look, but I was aware of a male couple kissing in a corner and a goth-like girl doing things to a skinhead. Al berated me as soon as he got me in there.

"What do you think you're doing?"

"What am *I* doing?" I answered back defiantly. "Why don't you ask that thing in the red dress and bovver boots! It's just beaten me black and blue!"

"That's Vendetta, the heaviest dominatrix on the scene! You're lucky to be *alive*!"

"Well, I didn't know, did I? It just suddenly came at me and started thrashing me with a cane!"

"They were playing *Bolero*! I told ye to scarper when they started playing *Bolero*! Only the hardcore come out for *Bolero*!"

"Oh, is *that* what it was?"

"And what about yer safe word? Why didn't you say yer safe word?"

"I *did*! I kept yelling it but it still wouldn't stop!"

"Did ye tell her it beforehand?"

"Sorry?"

"Yer safe word! Did ye tell her it beforehand?"

"Was I supposed to, then?"

He looked exasperated.

PAINFUL

"How's she supposed to know yer safe word if ye haven't told her it, ye daft prat!"

I was stumped for a response but not ready to concede.

"That's not the point! I came here for a life-changing experience. Ha! *Life-changing*? I've been propositioned by a 50-year-old baby who wanted his nappy changed, some floozy in a nurse's outfit who wanted to rub herself against my plaster casts, and a merciless thrashing at the hands of some creature that even David Attenborough would be hard-pressed to identify! And where were *you*, eh? You were gone for hours!"

"I was sending some fun up ma nose!" he answered defensively.

"Oh, yes, of course! Fun! That's all you ever think about, isn't it? Fun, fun, fun! Well, there's more to life than *fun*! And what about my drink? You were supposed to be buying me a drink!"

"Aye, I am!"

"So where *is* it?"

"I'm getting it in the noo!"

"Well, go on, then! I'm gasping here!"

"Right, then! Glass of red."

"Make it a large!"

He turned and wandered back inside, none too pleased.

"Bloody tight-arse Glaswegians!" I shouted after him.

It was the closest we'd come to an all-out row.

I sat there for a moment, resigned to another dreadful night when, without warning, the door opened and a woman entered. Tall, slender, with striking features. Raven-black hair to her shoulders, wearing a skin-tight black latex mini dress, deliberately tarty, but on her it looked incredible. Our eyes locked together and she came slowly, steadily towards me. She was quite

PAINFUL

simply stunning. Her skin and complexion were flawless, her body perfect. I could only stare at her, mesmerized. Even her voice was sublime. Soft, sensual, articulate.

"Are you sub or dom?" she asked alluringly.

"Sub," I answered, spellbound.

"Me too. Though I'm more into R and P."

"R and P?"

"Restraint and pleasure. Would you like to get to know me?"

"Yes, please."

She quietly got on top and carefully lowered herself onto me so as not to cause me any discomfort. There was nothing sordid or overt about it. Just two lives coming together. Divine intimacy.

"Do you come here often?" she smiled.

"My first time."

"Me too."

"What's your favourite film?"

It was a ridiculous thing to ask so soon after meeting her. I don't know why I said it. But she wasn't fazed, and her answer was perfect.

"West Side Story."

"Me too!"

She looked at me with warmth and tenderness.

"Te adoro, Anton."

"Te adoro, Maria."

And we both leant forward and kissed, soft, sensitive, surreal. That kiss – that kiss was the single most astonishing, most profound thing that had ever happened to me. It was like an explosion. I couldn't believe what was happening. It was like finding a place to belong. Heaven, pure and simple. And her smell – she smelt of eternity.

"You're the most beautiful woman I've ever seen."

"Thank you."
"What's your name?"
"Diane."
"Diane. Roman goddess of the moon."
"*Really*? I didn't know that."
"Also hunting and childbirth."
She laughed.
"Sounds like Angelina Jolie."
"What are you doing here? A woman like you. What's a woman like you doing in a place like this?"
She suddenly looked melancholy.
"I get lonely sometimes. Don't *you* get lonely sometimes?"
It was like she could see into my soul.
"Yes."
"I have money .... but no love. I have comfort .... but no warmth. Possessions .... but no joy."
"Who said that?" I asked in a daze.
She looked slightly confused.
"*I* did."
I realized I was saying some really stupid things.
"Why *me*?"
She put her hand on my cheek, smiled, and replied simply and directly.
"You have a kind face."
Our eyes never veered from one another. I felt I'd known her forever. Maybe a past life. Or the start of a new one. It was her – my soulmate. The one I'd waited my whole life for. How did I know? Because she saw it too.

I continued asking silly, banal questions. But each time she obliged with an answer, and each time it felt like a spiritual awakening.
"What's your favourite song?"
"Moon River."

PAINFUL

"Mine too."

"Breakfast At Tiffany's."

"I *love* that film!"

"Me too."

"Favourite food?"

"Chinese."

"Restaurant?"

"The Mandarin Swan in Chobham. It has a live fish tank."

"Can I take you there, Diane? Will you let me take you there and buy you the best meal ever?"

There was no hesitation.

"Yes. Of course. I'd love that."

She gently rose and opened a small shoulder bag that I hadn't noticed until then, brought out her lipstick, and wrote her phone number on one of the plaster casts.

"Call me," she said softly.

"You're not going?"

"I *have* to. I have work in the morning."

"No. *Please*. Don't go. I've waited so long to find you."

"Don't worry – we'll see each other again – if we're meant to."

She leant down and kissed my forehead. Then she quickly turned, opened the door, and she was gone. Back into the crowd, the whips and the chains, the carnal carnage, the weirdos and freaks. I sat in a stupor. I couldn't move or think.

The door opened again and Al came in with two drinks in plastic cups.

"Don't say I dinnae spoil ye!"

He held mine out for me to take, but I was still too much in shock. He stared into my pupils.

"Are you ok, boss?"

"No – not really."

"How no? What's happened?"
"I've met someone."
"Met someone?"
"I've met someone .... and I'm in love."
He stared at me in shock.
"*In love*?!"
"Her name's Diane. She's amazing and she's given me her phone number."
"You've met someone and you're in love. In the time it's taken for me to have a quick wee, go to the bar and get a drink .... you've met someone and you're in love."
"And I'm going to marry her."
His eyes suddenly bulged in dismay.
"MARRY HER?! Are ye off yer chump? Are ye away wi' the fucking fairies?! Listen, boss .... the people that come here .... they're not always what they seem, ya ken? They come, they play a part, then they go again. They dinnae come to a place like this to meet someone and fall in love!"
"I know what my heart's telling me, Al."
"But she could have been *anyone*! A tranny, a ladyboy, *anything*! She was probably on the game!"
I stared back at him, affronted.
"How *dare* you! Do you think I don't know when a woman is on the game?"
I thought about it.
"Well .... ok .... maybe not .... but I'm sure I would have *sensed* it. She was beautiful, she was intelligent, outgoing, charming ...."
"*Definitely* on the game! Did she give you her rates?"
Suddenly, from nowhere, someone shoved past us, I think it was the skinhead, nudged Al's shoulder, and the red wine went everywhere, mainly over me. Not just a drop, not just half of it, the entire cup! I looked down in horror – I was dripping!

"No! No!"

Then the door suddenly swung open with full force and the young sexy nurse reappeared, eyes manic, like she was about to burst apart with energy and was looking for an outlet. She immediately settled on me and came flying at me, landing on my legs, and started rubbing herself up and down my plaster casts again.

"No! Please! Get off!"

She ignored me and continued thrusting like a rampant dog on heat.

"Get her off me! Get her off me, Al! She's unhinged!"

By the time he'd pulled her off the damage was done. My plaster casts were soaked in wine stains. And Diane's phone number was smudged and smeared beyond recognition. I asked Al if he could make it out. He squinted and said it looked like the number of the clap clinic in Glasgow.

My life sank. It was gone. Gone forever.

17

Love. Everything feels new. Things smell fresh. You feel alive, awake, energized. Ordinary things take on a new meaning. Like brushing your teeth, going to the shops, having a bath. You see nature, you notice people. It's like a film that finally comes into focus. And you feel nothing can harm you. You're indestructible. Unless .... of course .... you've lost their phone number.

"Diane, Roman goddess of the moon ...."

"Better not say that."

"Why not?"

"She might've used a false name."

"How about .... the woman with the raven-black hair?"

"She might've been wearing a wig."

I rather resented Al's interference, but as I'd never done one of these internet messages before I felt I needed his help.

"The woman with the fabulous legs? She *must* have real legs!"

"What did she actually *say* to ye?"

"She said .... she said she got lonely sometimes .... and she was into 'R 'n' B'."

"*R 'n' B?*"

"No .... not R 'n' B .... M 'n' S?"

"That's a shop for rich cunts."

"K 'n' P! Yes – that was it – K 'n' P!"

Al looked doubtful.

"K 'n' P? Are you sure? I've never heard of it."

"That's definitely what she said."

"Ok. 'Good looking guy' ...."

"Gentleman. I prefer gentleman."

"Ok. 'Good looking gentleman wants to reconnect with the chick he met ....'"

"Lady. I think it should be lady."

"'The lady he met at the S 'n' M club.'"

"'You're into K 'n' P .... and your favourite restaurant is The Peking Duck in Cobham'."

"'If you'd like to carry on where we left off, FFS reply."

"FFS?"

"For fuck sake."

"'*Please* reply .... it will be lovely to hear from you.'"

"You don't need that last bit. It'll be more expensive."

"I can afford it. My last show was a hit."

"And don't put yer name on it. Say .... 'the guy with the magic plaster casts.'"

I changed that to 'the man from *West Side Story.*'

The final draft read:

'Good-looking gentleman would like to reconnect with lady of exotic beauty who 'gets lonely sometimes'. We met at the S and M club last week, you're into K and P, and your favourite restaurant is the Peking Duck in Cobham. If you'd like to carry on from where we left off and join me for a wonderful meal please reply. The man from West Side Story.'

I read it through a few times, then Al 'posted' it for me. Suddenly I was online.

18

The results were dismal. An entire week went by without a response.

Al came every day supposedly to finish the ramp, but spent most of the time sunbathing with his shirt off even though it was early March. The least glimmer of sun and he'd strip off, lie spread-eagled in the wheelbarrow, and fall asleep with his mouth open till he looked like a dead lobster.

Morag continued to do the shopping and the housework, but Al kept pondering ways of getting rid of her once and for all. Since chaining her to the radiator for a whole day and night he was becoming increasingly desperate. He'd seriously considered the following methods: dumping her on the M1, hanging her upside down from a tree, making her sleep in the cement mixer, and trying to sell her at a car boot sale.

Then, Monday morning at nine o' clock, I checked my phone and I nearly died of shock. Diane had replied!

'Yes, would like to carry on at The Peking Duck in Cobham, my favourite restaurant. Wednesday at 8?'

I couldn't believe it! I immediately booked a table and prepared to meet my soulmate.

I'd never felt so nervous in all my life! Even my wedding to Yvette at Kingston registry office wasn't as stomach-churning.

I wore my dinner suit and dickie bowtie as I figured the restaurant must be incredibly exclusive given Diane's elegance and class. The only problem was I couldn't get the bottom of the trousers over my plaster casts so I had to cut them up the sides. They looked a bit odd but it was better than a tuxedo and tracksuit bottoms. Even Al got dressed up, looking quite smart in a slightly crumpled suit that he'd acquired from Oxfam.

I also decided to use my crutches for the first time rather than the wheelchair as I wanted to look 'cool', something which had mostly eluded me throughout my 53 years. It still hurt to stand, but the pain was gradually subsiding, which showed I was slowly on the mend in spite of being attacked by Vendetta and a deranged sexy nurse. The future suddenly looked bright.

As we arrived in Cobham my heart started to pound. We reached the high street and there it was – The Peking Duck, Cantonese Cuisine. From the exterior it looked smart and stylish, with the name in big neon lights.

We were able to park directly outside as Al had nicked a disabled badge from someone. I didn't approve and told him so, but had to admit it did come in rather handy.

I opened the car door, hoisted myself up on the crutches, then hopped to the entrance like Long John Silver. To my slight consternation, Al followed.

"Are you going in?" I asked in a way that said *please don't*.

"Aye, I'm starving!" he answered chirpily. Then he just stood there.

"Well, open the bloody door, then!" I barked.

He opened the door and we both entered.

It was spacious, around fifty tables, all laid out and ready for service. There was a large tropical fish tank down the middle, dividing the restaurant into two halves. I pointed excitedly.

"Look! The fish tank that she spoke about!"

Then I looked around and it was empty. Completely deserted. Not a soul. I dismissed it and decided it didn't matter – just being with Diane would be enough.

A runt-like waiter came running towards us with a massive grin. He was wearing a large, ill-fitting dinner jacket over a rather grubby shapeless white shirt and bowtie similar to my own, except his was wonky. He stood around five foot and his hair was smarmed back with Brylcreem. He had enormous protruding teeth and was holding a soiled tea-towel over his arm.

"You booked?" he asked enthusiastically, beaming from ear to ear.

"Yes, I have a table booked for eight o' clock in the name of May."

"Just minute .... I look in book."

And he actually opened the reservations book to check whether there was a table or not.

"Hah, yeah. Table for two booked in name of May. Follow me!"

He turned and led us to a table near the back. I hobbled after him while Al stopped to examine the fish tank.

"Oi, mate! This fish tank's fucking dead!"

"Eh?"

"*Dead*!"

"*Dead*? How you know?"

"*How I know*? The water's thick green and there's a dead fish floating on top!"

The waiter suddenly roared with laughter, shoulders shaking with joviality.

"Ha, yeah! It broke!"

"Well, I suggest you get it fixed!" Al rebuked. "Fish are fucking human too, ya know!"

PAINFUL

I was slightly taken aback. I had no idea he was so fond of fish. The waiter pulled out a chair and I sat. I got the sense we were the only customers he'd seen in a long time.

"Drink? You want drink?" he asked keenly.

"No, thanks. I'll wait till my guest arrives."

At which point Al sat down opposite, picked up the menu and started to study it, totally at ease.

"Drink? You want drink?"

"Aye."

The waiter looked confused.

"Eh?"

Al looked up and a cultural clash ensued.

"*Aye.*"

"Aye?"

"*Aye*! A pinta lager."

"Nose."

"Eh?"

"Eye, nose, ear."

"*Lager*! Ah'll have a pinta *lager*!"

"Eh?"

"*Lager*! A fucking pinta lager!"

The waiter roared.

"You speak funny!"

He turned and went into the kitchen with Al staring after him in amazement.

"My Christ, what an ugly cunt!" he exclaimed.

Then he carried on looking at the menu, relaxed and settled. I cleared my throat and tried to be as subtle as I could.

"Yes. Listen .... Al .... I'm on a date."

He looked oblivious.

"Ey, dinnae mind me, boss. I'm cool with it. The two of yeez just crack on, ye won't even know I'm here!"

"No .... the thing is .... we hardly know each other. We've only met the once. There's a lot to find out. I think it would be better if you sat at another table."

His face fell. He looked hurt.

"Eh?"

"If you don't mind."

"Ye want me to sit at another table?"

"Yes, please."

He seemed genuinely upset.

"Aye. Sure. If that's what ye want. I'd hate to embarrass you in front of yer lady friend, know what I mean? Being an ex-convict an' aw."

He rose with that now familiar hangdog expression and went to another table nearby. I almost felt guilty for not wanting him to intrude on my love life and eavesdrop on our conversation.

Suddenly the door opened and a woman appeared. Now when I say *woman*, what I actually mean is someone in a woolly bobble-hat, woolly gloves, duffel coat and thick horn-rimmed glasses. To say she was plain would be a bit of an understatement. Like calling Quasimodo a bit of a hunchback. Not *ugly* exactly – more '*ordinary*'. She looked like a train spotter with a bent for bird watching.

The waiter suddenly rushed in from the kitchen, ecstatic.

"Aw, we busy tonight!" he yelled, and ran up to her excitedly.

They exchanged words and I saw him look inside the reservations book. Next thing I know, she's coming slowly, steadily towards me looking like someone about to do a bungy-jump. My heart, mouth and stomach all fell at the same time, like they were in an elevator plunging to its death. It couldn't be – *could* it? She arrived at the table with a nervous smile.

PAINFUL

"Are you the man from West Side Story?" she asked tentatively.

I looked up at her, desperately trying to conceal my disappointment.

"You must be the exotic beauty who gets lonely sometimes," I answered deadpan.

She nodded.

"You better sit down."

She sat, looking highly embarrassed. The waiter reappeared behind her.

"Drink? You want drink?"

"No – not yet," I answered. "Unless *you* do, er ...."

"Jane."

"Jane."

"Tea? You want tea?" the waiter asked keenly.

"No, not at the moment, thank you," I replied.

"But it free."

"Sorry?"

"Tea free."

"Oh – tea *free*."

"Yeah – tea free!"

"No, thanks."

"But it *free*! Tea *free*!"

"Yes, but we don't want it."

"But it *free*!"

I finally gave up and gave in.

"Alright, then – we'll have the tea."

"But you have to have food wiv it. Uvverwise it not free!"

By now I was worn-out.

"Fine! Bring us the bloody tea, even though we don't want it, and if we don't eat anything I'll pay for it at the end!"

He nodded and grinned, teeth protruding more than ever, and went back into the kitchen.

PAINFUL

Jane looked bewildered and confused.

"Shall I ...." she asked awkwardly.

"Sorry?"

"Take off my ...."

"Oh – yes – *yes,* of course!"

She stood up again, unbuttoned her duffel coat and took it off, revealing a long grey pleated skirt, sandals, rather garish woollen socks, and an incredibly thick woolly jumper with a frolicking sheep on the front. She placed the coat on the back of her chair and sat down again to face me. She removed her gloves but kept her woolly hat on. I tried to make pleasant small talk.

"So .... this is your favourite restaurant."

"Well .... it *was*. It's not quite what it was. It used to be packed. I think it must be under new management."

At which point Al suddenly shouted over from the other table.

"Ey, boss! Have ye checked out the set meal for two? You get the soup, the mixed starters, chicken 'n' cashew nuts, sweet 'n' sour pork, and the egg fried rice all for twenty quid! Might be good for you an' the missus, eh?"

I ignored the idiot.

"So .... Jane .... there's obviously been a misunderstanding. I put out an advert *specifically* citing certain things, like S 'n' M, K 'n' P, the man from West Side Story etcetera .... which you answered."

"Yes. It seemed so *appropriate*! It all made perfect sense! All the pieces seemed to fit!"

I looked at her incredulously.

"S 'n' M?"

"My favourite pastime."

"Forgive me .... but you don't seem the sort."

"Oh, yes! I couldn't live without my S 'n' M!"

"Bondage? Torture?"

PAINFUL

She suddenly looked mystified.

"*Torture*? No! Knitting!"

"*Knitting*?"

"Yes! I belong to a knitting club. The S 'n' M Club of Eastcote!"

Yes – it was true – she actually belonged to a knitting club in Eastcote called the S 'n' M club where they took along their knitting to show each other and discuss their next project. S 'n' M stood for *Stitch And Make*.

"And K 'n' P?"

"Knit and purl," she said with expert knowledge. "Knit and purl are the first stitches you learn when you start. Obviously the knit stitch comes first – *nothing* happens in knitting without the knit stitch – but as we say at the club, 'Once you've mastered the knit stitch, it's time to get your purl on'!"

She laughed hysterically, actually believing this to be highly hilarious. I tried to laugh with her but my heart just wasn't in it. I felt like I'd been tossed into the air by a large horse. She then went on to elaborate about all the other stitches you can learn – the rib stitch, the moss stitch, otherwise known as the seed stitch, the SSK stitch, the kitchener stitch, not to mention the stockinette stitch – and all the wonderful things you can go on to make with them.

"I've knitted virtually everything I've got on," she beamed with pride. "This jumper .... my gloves .... my hat .... even my socks!"

I sat and marvelled at how boring she was.

At this point another Chinese man came out, almost identical to the first, only this one was wearing battered jeans and an old t-shirt under a soiled apron. He came up to us holding a drink.

"Pinta lager?"

"No, the other table. We ordered tea."

"Yeah. My bruvver making it."

"Well, where *is* it? It's been ages!"

"Yeah – he making it."

"How many people does it take to make tea and pour a lager in an empty restaurant?" I queried, genuinely perplexed.

He went to the other table with Jane now on a roll, waffling on unabated.

"Now .... out of all the garments I'm wearing .... what do you think was the hardest one to knit?"

I tried to look interested but my brain had gone to sleep and I was far more engrossed in the conversation happening at the other table.

"Pinta lager?"

Al was staring at him, mock-astounded.

"Fuck me, *you're* ugly an' aw!"

The waiter's brother laughed uncontrollably, shoulders shaking with gleefulness.

"Yeah!"

"You're even uglier than the *other* cunt!"

"Yeah! We're bruvvers. Him waiter, me chef!"

"*Brothers*? Did yer mother mate with a blobfish or something?"

The chef roared.

"I tell ye, I've seen some ugly fuckers in my time, son, but you two take the fucking biscuit!"

"Yeah!" he agreed, shoulders shaking again.

Unfortunately, I was drawn back by Jane who was now in full knitting mode.

"*Most* people would say the jumper because it's the largest item. *Wrong*! The jumper was actually quite easy. A fairly simple straightforward stockinette and garter stitch. No – the hardest thing to knit was actually the socks! Firstly, you've got the cuff and leg – then

PAINFUL

you've got the heel flap – and finally you've got the 'grafting the toe' ...."

I had to intervene, otherwise we'd have been there till another customer arrived and that could have been weeks.

"So .... Jane .... sorry to rush you .... but how did you come to answer the advert?"

"Ah – well – yes – that's a very interesting story ...."

It turned out that a man had attended the knitting class, which was highly unusual because it's mostly all women. Asian, apparently. Anyway, Jane started to show him how to knit, their eyes met, and a strange feeling ran through her, like dropping a stitch and finding it again. Then the class finished and he left without leaving a contact number. She didn't even find out his name. Looking at her, I wasn't surprised.

"And *'the man from West Side Story'*?"

"He told me he'd played the piano in an amateur production."

I felt obliged to buy her a meal. And, of course, Al ordered everything on the menu. And I found out that if you want to add stripes, which is a great way of brightening up your knitting, you have to be aware that there are lots of pesky ends to sew in afterwards.

19

For the next few days I went into a decline. Not a depression exactly, but certainly a bit of a low. I hardly left my bedroom. She'd gone, I knew it. There was no way of finding her. My only hope was that she might turn up at the next Skin Club session in three weeks' time, but I knew it was a longshot. And even if she *did*, I wasn't sure if she'd speak to me given that I hadn't phoned her. Despair filled my head and my heart. I couldn't see the point in getting up. And I *still* hadn't managed to cut my toenails.

On the third day of my malaise, at around 12 noon, I suddenly became aware of some sort of commotion going on at the back of the cottage. Someone screaming. I dismissed it at first as this had become a fairly regular occurrence. Then I heard Al drive off, then Morag pathetically calling for help. I tutted and cursed, pulled myself up from the bed, and began the long slow trek to the guest bedroom at the back. I was starting to hobble now, but it hurt every time I landed.

It was a horrid, foul day, dark, cloudy, with a nasty, steady drizzle. I opened the window and looked out to find Morag pinned to a tree in her underwear, cold, wet and frightened.

"Morag?"
"Aye, it's me!"
"What's happening? Why are you screaming?"
"Ah'm tied to a tree! Ah cannae move!"
"Where's Al?"

PAINFUL

"Gone off somewhere in his motor. He made me strip then tied us up. He's got something planned, ah know it!"

"For god's sake, has he got nothing better to do on a Saturday?" I complained.

"D'ye think ye could come 'n' untie us, please, Brian? It's freezing oot here. Ma nipples have gone all hard! They're standing tae attention, so they are! Ah need tae warm 'um up!"

I was a bit miffed because I'd wanted to spend the whole day in bed wallowing in self-pity.

"Ok – hang on!"

Although my legs were definitely on the mend, it was still a bloody nightmare getting downstairs, into the wheelchair, and out into the garden – especially if you needed a wee, which I did. Without going into details, I obviously still couldn't stand up so I had to go sitting down like a lady, and I swear I will *never* criticize women ever again for taking too long. It's an extremely hazardous and delicate procedure, believe you me!

So I went for a wee. Then, of course, I realized I was still in my pyjamas and had to go back to the bedroom to get my dressing gown, and as I was removing it from the wardrobe I heard Al's car returning.

I looked out and saw him alight, followed by the waiter and the chef from the restaurant the other night, and two raggedy old vagrants who looked like they hadn't washed in years. Al turned and addressed them like some stiff-backed army sergeant major about to go into battle.

"Ok, lads – this is it! Form an orderly line and no jumping the queue! You'll all get a turn!"

The four of them stared back at him, deadpan.

"You can do her up the jack 'n' danny or up the old deaf 'n' dumb, whichever one you prefer. Take yer time

.... enjoy yerselves .... and I can put a bag over her head if that'll help. Any questions?"

"Where's the cider?" asked one of the vagrants gruffly.

"Yeah, where's the cider?" demanded the other.

"You said you'd give us some cider if we humped her."

"You ain't humped her yet, have ye!" answered Al aggressively.

"Hump her? What that?" asked the Chinese chef to the Chinese waiter.

"Rumpy-pumpy!" grinned the Chinese waiter, gesticulating with his fist and laughing.

"Ha. Yeah. Rumpy-pumpy!" laughed the chef, also raising his fist.

"Right, men – follow me!"

And he led them around the side of the cottage and into the back garden. I was beside myself.

I hopped to the stairlift, got downstairs and into the wheelchair as fast as I could, then over to the French windows to find poor Morag trembling in fear.

"No! No! Not the down-and-outs, Ally, *please* not the down-and-outs!"

"Right! The chinkies go first!" he bellowed, as if arranging an audition for 'Britain's Got Talent'.

I opened the doors and yelled at the top of my voice.

"AL!"

He froze in his tracks before breaking into his usual conciliatory smile.

"Howdy, boss. Howzitgoan? Thought you'd be in yer bed all depressed, like."

I'd been angry with him before, but never anything like this. I clenched my teeth and roared at him.

"What the hell do you think you're *doing*!"

"Just introducing Morag to some of ma new pals."

PAINFUL

"Untie her at once and bring her inside to get warm! And get these people off my property!"

To my amazement, Al's 'guests' responded with downright indignation.

"What about the cider?"

"Yeah, what about the cider?"

"What about rumpy-pumpy?"

"Yeah, what about rumpy-pumpy?"

"Tough! Go! Leave! Before I call the police!"

The two vagrants looked at one another, then begrudgingly started to leave to return to wino corner or wherever the hell Al had picked them up from.

"Bloody disgrace," moaned one of them.

"And did you clock the bloody state of her?" said the other.

Poor Morag looked even more demoralised.

"Well, don't just stand there, UNTIE HER!" I snapped.

He began to loosen the rope which he'd attached to the tree.

"How we gonna get to station?" the Chinese waiter demanded to know.

"Yeah, we gotta get back to restaurant for lunchtime rush?" added the brother.

"It Saturday. Saturdays very busy!"

"Do a right out of here, then a left, then another right, walk up the high street, past Boots, and you'll come to a bloody taxi rank. Now skedaddle!" I shouted, unmoved.

They looked at each other, then reluctantly left.

"Right! You two! Inside! NOW!" I demanded.

The two of them came gingerly in, Morag cold and bedraggled, Al now looking decidedly sheepish.

"Morag, are you alright?"

"Jis a wee bit shivery," she said wretchedly.

"Why don't you go upstairs and run yourself a nice hot bath? You'll find a kimono-type thing that Yvette left behind in the wardrobe. You can wear that."

She lowered her head and nodded, still highly humiliated and on the verge of tears. She made her way to the stairs and, to my slight consternation, used the stairlift and started to ascend. It creaked and groaned under her weight. I thought it was going to collapse. I watched her disappear, then turned and glared at Al like an irate parent.

"So! What have you got to say for yourself?"

At which point he crumbled like a naughty schoolboy caught masturbating in the toilets.

"I'm sorry, boss! I'm *so* fucking sorry! Oh, God! Oh, God, forgive me! I ken it was wrong! But I was *desperate*! I didnae know what else to do! The woman just won't take a hint!"

"*My* house! *My* garden!" I chided bitterly.

"I know. It's fucking unforgivable! I'd 've dunnit in ma *own* garden but I dinnae have one. I don't even have ma own bathroom. I have to share with illegal immigrants an' they're none too toilet savvy, I can tell ye!"

But I wasn't ready to let it go.

"*My* property! How could you bring those people onto *my* property?! And what about Morag? That's akin to *rape*!"

"Nah, I wouldnae let 'em go through with it! It was just to scare her off a bit, like!"

"It was a disgusting and despicable thing to do!"

He hung his head in shame.

"Aye – you're right. I don't know what's wrong wi' me, boss. I haven't been maself of late. I think I might be going through the menopause. I'm all over the fucking shop!"

PAINFUL

He now seemed as upset as Morag, and against my better judgement I told him to sit, turned the wheelchair to face him, and decided to give him another chance to explain himself.

"Okay. Let's hear it. Why do you think you do what you do? Why do you think you behave in such an odious and malignant way?"

"What's that mean?"

"Nasty and evil."

He lowered his eyes and slowly began to offload, obviously recalling some extremely painful memories.

"I think it goes all the way back to ma childhood in the Gorbals, boss. Eight of us in a two-bed high rise, six kids in the same bed. Ma da was a dealer, ma maw was on the game. Used to bring the clients back while we was trying to sleep. Ma cunt of an older brother used to use ma face as a football. Ma big sis sold blow-jobs to ma mates for a fiver. The other three hated me coz I was always the clever one. The only thing that ever showed me any love was ma dog Jock."

"I didn't know you had a dog?" I said quietly.

"Aye. Jock was a big old sloppy mongrel, loyal as fuck. A stray. I found him wandering in the street one day and brought him home. He was devoted to me. Used to sleep in the same bed as us."

"With six other people?" I gaped.

"Aye. There was always room for big Jock. Then one day, hungry as he was, Jock ate ma da's new cannabis plant by mistake. The poor fucker was out of it for a week. When ma da found out he went totally ballistic. An' he strangled poor Jock to death in front of me. Then he laid his dead body at ma feet and told me I'd never have another pet coz I couldn't look after 'em. The only thing I ever truly loved and who loved me.

Gone. An' that's when I turned against the world an' railed against society."

I was almost taken-in. He was a convincing actor. But then I pulled myself together.

"Sorry .... but what's your dog Jock got to do with tying Morag to a tree and threatening to molest her?"

"Right 'n' wrong, boss. I never learnt it. It was never taught us."

I relented. It was probably true – he'd probably had the sort of upbringing where right and wrong meant what kind of sauce you had with your fish and chips.

"Ok. Here's what's going to happen. I'm going to hire Morag as my permanent housekeeper and you will *not* go anywhere near her. Do you understand? No more chaining her to the radiator, no more tying her to trees, leaving her out in the cold .... from now on you will treat her with dignity and respect. You can stay on as my personal chauffeur and dog's body until my plaster casts come off, hopefully in the next few weeks. *Then*, Al .... we part company!"

He looked sad and humbled.

"What about the ramp?"

"The ramp?"

"Aye. Don't ye want us to finish it?"

I stared at him aghast.

"The *ramp*? You said it would take 24 hours – it's been almost two months!"

"Aye, but .... other things have come up."

"Yes, like tying Morag to a tree!"

"I'll finish it. I promise. I'll finish it today."

"A: I won't *need* a bloody ramp once the plaster casts come off! And B: I could have bought one on the internet for less than a hundred! One of those nice, neat, ready-made jobs that you fold up and store in your garage when you don't need it. So far it's cost me an

PAINFUL

absolute fortune! Not to mention the bloody eyesore I have to wake up to every day!"

To give him his due, he worked like a trojan for the rest of the afternoon. The cement mixer went nonstop, I watched him going back and forth with the wheelbarrow, and he even seemed to know what he was doing. He almost looked professional as he smoothed the concrete with a steel trowel. He continued until after dark, eventually finishing around 7.

He came back the next day to proudly show it off to me, pushing me outside so I could test-drive it. Unfortunately the cement was still soft, the wheelchair got stuck, and I was there for forty-five minutes while he tried to yank me out. In the end he had to carry me on his shoulder, complaining of chest pains and shortage of breath, before putting me down and lighting another roll-up. He then spent the rest of the day trying to remove the wheelchair from the cement without success. The *next* day he had to hire a large pneumatic drill to smash it all up again, another £54.15p + VAT. The noise was horrendous and by the end of it he was still shuddering, looking like he'd suddenly developed St Vitus Dance. And the wheelchair would never be quite the same again. Both wheels felt buckled, which meant I'd probably lose my £100 deposit.

It was then I realized the man was a complete and utter prat!

20

How I let him talk me into it I'll never know. I must have been mad. A fetish party in Hersham. My gut instinct told me to avoid it like the plague. It sounded dodgy beyond belief. I imagined Satanists, naked butlers, men in drag. It could only lead to another disaster. But he somehow managed to persuade me that Diane might be there, even though I knew she wouldn't be. A woman like her at a fetish party in Hersham? It didn't quite sound right. But after the last two months or so, *anything* was possible.

"So what does a fetish party actually consist of?" I asked him as we were driving there.

"People with fetishes," he answered vaguely.

"Yes, but .... I mean .... what's going to happen? What can I expect to see?"

He thought about it.

"People with fetishes."

We arrived in the middle of a council estate; identical blocks of flats, 6-7 floors high, about as enticing as a holiday on death row. It was badly lit and sort of creepy. No one about, just these stark grey buildings.

We slowly drove around looking for the right place. Narrow winding lanes with parked cars either side, crammed into small spaces. Every now and then we'd reach a dead end and have to go back on ourselves. It was like a maze. But still no actual person in sight.

We eventually found it – Block H, flats 11-76. We parked on the pavement which Al felt intitled to do because of the disabled badge. He then marched towards the building with me on my crutches struggling to keep up.

We reached the communal entrance, he pressed the intercom, we heard it come on, followed by silence.

"Operation Mindwarp," Al said into the intercom.

I felt an instant cold shiver go down my spine. *Operation Mindwarp*? It just disn't sound right.

We heard a click and the thick glass door opened. We entered into a cold, dank lobby with a stairwell and a single lift. It smelt of urine and disinfectant. We pressed for the lift and waited.

"*Operation Mindwarp?*" I queried, perturbed.

"Aye, that's the password. Ye cannae get in without a password."

"Yes, but .... *why* Operation Mindwarp?"

He shrugged dismissively.

"How the fuck should I know?"

"Supposed to be a party, isn't it?"

"So?"

"Doesn't sound very party-like, does it?"

"What do you want, '*Jolly Festivities*'?"

"Just sounds a bit ominous, that's all," I quivered as the lift approached.

"What's that mean?"

"Threatening."

"Fear no, big mon. I'm there to protect ye. I willnae let the brain-sucking green aliens abduct yeez!"

The lift doors opened and we entered. Al pressed for the seventh floor and we slowly began to ascend. It was one of those slow, creaky old lifts you fully expect to break down at any moment. Someone had graffitied **REHAB IS FOR QUITTERS** on one side, and **CONSTIPATED BUT NO ONE GIVES A SHIT** on the other.

I felt an overwhelming sense of foreboding as we neared the top. It seemed to take forever. We reached the seventh, found the flat, and Al knocked. The door slowly opened and a man peered out at us suspiciously. I was immediately spooked. Not because he looked like a Satanist, but because he looked so *ordinary*! Bland beyond belief! Fiftyish, shortish, pale-ish. Bald on top with about half a dozen hideously long hairs placed strategically across his scalp. What we used to call, when I was a kid, a 'Bobby Charlton'. And to cap it all he was wearing a dressing gown, striped pyjamas and slippers. He looked ready for bed! He stared at us vacuously with large, saucer-like eyes without saying a word.

"Operation Mindwarp," Al repeated.

The man stepped back to allow us in, closed the door behind us, then went into a nearby room, leaving us in the hall to find our own way. The flat, like the man, was small, drab and utterly bland. And there was nothing but silence. No music, no sounds of people or conversation, just an eerie lack of noise.

"Right. I'm gonna find the bog. You go in an' introduce yerself an' I'll join yeez in a mo."

I immediately started to panic.

"*Me*? Go in there alone? What am I going to say?"

"Just be yer usual outgoing, witty self."

And with that he waltzed off, opening the doors to the other rooms until he found the toilet and disappeared. I took a deep breath and ventured in there on my crutches.

Half a dozen people were sitting in a circle on the floor, including the man in pyjamas. They all looked sort of dead, completely static as if frozen in time, focused on absolutely nothing, not even each other. I just stood there, not knowing what to say or do. No one

PAINFUL

acknowledged my presence. So I told the only joke I knew.

"Do you know what the number one cause of divorce is?"

No one answered.

"Marriage."

But no one laughed. Nothing – not even a titter. A complete embarrassing non-reaction. I'd never felt so awkward in all my life, and that was saying something! Here was someone who needed the loo in the middle of *Schindler's List*, spilt someone's popcorn on the way, and made an horrendous crunching noise on my return just as 200 people were about to be gassed. As embarrassing as it was, it was *nothing* compared to the vibe in that room. Thankfully I saw an unoccupied sofa and headed straight for it.

I sat there for several minutes. It was excruciating. Absolutely nothing happened. Just utter inertia. Then I noticed a young couple squatting on the floor the other side. A man in his twenties, possibly Indian, and a young girl of 17 or 18. He was dark and swarthy with long, black, slicked-back hair. She was petite, blonde and pretty. They were the only people who looked 'dressed up' for the occasion. He was wearing one of those Saturday Night Fever suits, brilliant white with wide lapels, a waistcoat and flared trousers with a contrasting black shirt; she was all in black, with vivid red lipstick, a small revealing top, a mini skirt, bare legs and stilettos. They were both staring over at me, smoking what I now knew to be a joint.

Eventually Al burst in, ebullient. He saw the gathering of zombies on the floor and sneered derisively.

"Fuck me, belter of a party this, eh? Ah seen more life up a nun's fucking clouts!"

He rolled his shoulders, then came strutting over and sat next to me on the sofa. His movements were fast and jerky. He was sniffing a lot and his right leg wouldn't stop twitching. I ignored it, more concerned with the strange behaviour of the people in the room.

"What's wrong with them?" I hissed so they wouldn't hear me.

"They're on ket," he said matter-of-factly without lowering his voice.

"Ket?"

"Ketamine. I've seen people on it before. They go into their own fucking mental asylum."

"What is it?"

"Horse tranquilizer."

My mouth fell open in shock.

"*What?*"

"They also use it to stun elephants."

"No!"

"Shittiest drug known to man. Boring as fuck."

He then reached into his combat jacket and brought out some white powder in a see-through plastic envelope, stuck his fingers in, and snorted some up his nose.

"What's that? Not that cocaine stuff again, is it?" I asked disapprovingly.

"A wee bit o' speed," he sniffed, immediately more edgy. "Bumps up the old adrenalin."

Before I could react, the guy in the white suit appeared and perched next to Al on the arm of the sofa. He offered his joint, which Al took without comment and began smoking like it was his own.

"I'm Vinnie."

"No shit," replied Al, unimpressed.

PAINFUL

There was something about Vinnie that was instantly repellent. Everything about him was obnoxious. His clothes, his hair, his oily skin. His cocky manner, the arrogant smirk, even the way he sat. It was immediate. Misogyny dripped from every pore. You couldn't help but recoil.

"That's my wife Chloe," he said, nodding towards the girl on the other side of the room. Al looked.

"Cute."

"Like her?"

"Aye, she's a doll."

"Great lay an' all."

"I bet."

"Wanna fuck her?"

Al looked again, now with more interest.

"Sure, why not?" he shrugged.

"I'll let you fuck her."

"That's big o' ya."

"But I wanna watch."

Al now turned to stare at Vinnie with a mix of mild amusement and controlled disdain.

"You want me to fuck yer wife .... an' you wanna watch."

"Yeah."

"Here?"

"Our place."

"Where's that?"

"Five minute drive from here."

Al considered it for a moment.

"Ok, let's go," he said and rose.

21

We got outside and made our way to Al's car. Vinnie was already waiting, engine running. He had one of those incredibly flash sports cars, I think it was a Ferrari, bright red with gaudy bumpers and headlights. He obviously had money, but it was probably as dodgy as his breath.

Vinnie set off and we followed. He drove at a slow, even pace to make sure we didn't lose him. We left the council estate and came onto a well-lit main road. From the back of the car I watched Al reach into his combat jacket, bring out a hip flask, and take a large swig of what I assumed was scotch. Speed, a joint, and now scotch. I wanted to be a million miles away. All I saw ahead was a horror show. But *nothing* could have prepared me for what actually occurred.

We entered another estate, full of new-build maisonettes. It was exactly the sort of pad you'd have predicted for someone like Vinnie. Showy, modern, overpriced. We arrived and watched as he and his 'wife' entered their property, Vinnie deliberately leaving the door ajar.

Al reached under the passenger seat and brought out an enormous roll of clingfilm. I was mystified. He read my mind.

"Industrial. Take it with me everywhere. Never know when it might come in handy."

He left the car and headed towards the maisonette with the clingfilm under his arm. I didn't *have* to go, I could have stayed in the car. But I didn't fancy sitting there for God knows how long and, if I'm being honest, a part of me was intrigued.

PAINFUL

We went into a large, open-plan living room full of ostentatious furnishings and pictures of Vinnie everywhere. Centre piece was a curved retro cocktail bar with a leopard print front and Formica top. A massive widescreen TV with white leather seats all around, thick cream carpet, and a gauche burgundy sideboard with built-in lighting. Like Vinnie, it was too much. It made you feel ill.

Al sauntered in as if he owned the place. Vinnie was standing there expectantly with no sign of Chloe. He saw me and looked put-out.

"What's *he* doing here?"

"He's come to watch," Al answered flippantly. "Ye don't mind that, do ya, Vinnie? *You* wanna watch, *he* wants to watch, everyone wants to watch. It's a world of fucking watchers! So where's that cute little wife o' yours?"

"Getting changed. I told her to wear something 'appropriate'."

"*Always* does what you tell her, does she?"

"Yeah – I control her."

"Oh, you *control* her."

"Yeah, the stupid bitch ain't got a clue."

Al gave him a long, steady, menacing look, then put the clingfilm down on the burgundy sideboard.

"What's that for?" asked Vinnie, curious.

Al ignored him.

"Get me a drink."

"Eh?"

Al suddenly yelled belligerently.

"Get me a fucking drink, ya cunt!"

Vinnie, somewhat taken aback, went obediently to the cocktail bar while Al looked nonchalantly around.

"We're .... we're a bit low on booze," Vinnie said, slightly uncomfortable. "We're more into drugs. We've got crème de menthe or Baileys."

Al looked disgusted.

"*Crème de menthe or Baileys*?! You a fucking buftie or something?! What kinda fucking bar you running here, ya cunt! Got any charlie?"

"No – just weed."

"You're a fucking lightweight, son! A fucking faggot o' the first fucking order, ya cunt yeez!"

He brought out his hip flask and had another large, aggressive swig. I watched in awe. Oh, my God. This was happening. This was actually happening. I'd never seen him so truculent.

"One other thing ...." said Vinnie.

"What's that?"

"I want you to hit her."

Al suddenly went weirdly still and stared at him with strange intent.

"You want me to fuck yer wife while you're watching, and you want me to hit her while I'm fucking her."

"Yeah."

"Don't want much, do ya, pal?"

"It turns me on."

"What about her? Does it turn *her* on?"

"She does whatever I tell her."

Al now brought out the bag of speed, sprinkled some onto his hand, and had another long deep snort.

The door opened and Chloe entered, now wearing a beige satin camisole top and panties to match. She stood in front of Al as if asking for his approval. He saw her and immediately broke into a broad, lecherous grin.

"Oh, *yeah*! Rock 'n' roll, darling!"

PAINFUL

He strutted over to her, grabbed her, and stuck his tongue down her throat. She responded. To my amazement she began stroking his hair and pushing herself up against him. It was odd seeing a girl of her age snogging a guy approaching sixty. Vinnie stared on, mesmerized. It went on for about a minute before Al finally broke off to admire the view.

"Oh, Chloe – what *I* am gonna do for *you*!"

Then his hand went straight up the inside of her bare legs to her vagina which he began caressing. She instantly became aroused. My jaw dropped. I could barely believe what I was seeing. Vinnie came from behind the bar and watched, absorbed. But Al kept his eyes totally on Chloe, breathing seductively down her neck while he continued touching her.

"You're beautiful, babe, ya know that? Dead horny an' aw. I'm hard just looking at yeez. So what ye into? Rough, *really* rough, or just a straight, hard, consistent pounding?"

Vinnie suddenly interjected.

"The bedroom."

Al stopped, turned and stared at him, crazy-eyed.

"*Eh?*"

"I want you to fuck her in the bedroom. There's a camera up there."

Al glanced back at Chloe apologetically.

"'Scuse me a minute, sweetheart."

He released her, strode boldly over to Vinnie, grabbed him by his lapels, threw him against the wall, and growled in his face.

"Listen, ye motherfucking lightweight piece o' shite! It's not about what *you* want, ya ken?! No one gives a fuck what *you* want! You're nothing, you're superfluous! You're just a fucking spectator! It's about what *I* want and what *she* wants, ya got it?!"

Vinnie just gawked, speechless.

"Face the wall," Al suddenly commanded.

Vinnie's eyes went blank. He seemed almost transfixed.

"You hear what I said? Face the fucking wall!"

"But I wanna watch," he said feebly.

With no preamble, Al clenched his teeth and punched Vinnie hard in the stomach. Vinnie let out a long stifled yell and doubled over. Al pulled him back up by his hair and bellowed in his face.

"How *dare* you disobey me!"

He then hit him with full force in the face, sending him reeling across the room and collapsing in a heap, with blood pouring from his nose and mouth onto the cream carpet. Al followed him, unmoved, and kicked him in the ribs for good measure.

I tried to speak but couldn't. I'd never seen anyone hit before. It was horrible. Deeply disturbing. Like a road accident. You don't want to watch but you can't turn away. Bone against flesh. Everything landed with a sickening thud. I was repulsed. But not enough to stop the carnage that was taking place right in front of me. As for Al, he was in his element. He was Big Al McFadden, all-male, all-powerful, in complete control and loving every minute of it. He turned his attention back to Chloe.

"Where's the bathroom, babe?"

She looked totally unfazed by the violence.

"There's two. One downstairs and an en-suite upstairs," she said compliantly.

"Go to the one downstairs. Run a cold bath. I'll be with you in a minute."

She nodded and left. Al returned to Vinnie and nudged him with his foot. Vinnie slowly opened his eyes.

PAINFUL

"Get up," Al ordered coldly.

Vinnie, now with total fear on his face, gradually pulled himself up and stood on unsteady legs.

"Strip."

"Eh?"

"STRIP!"

Vinnie, too scared to refuse, removed his jacket, unbuttoned his shirt and began to strip while Al had another snort of speed.

"Not yer skiddies," he said without looking. "No one wants to see that pathetic wee tadger o' yours!"

Another snort, another swig from the hip flask, and Vinnie was down to his underpants. Al now picked up the industrial clingfilm, sauntered back, and began to wrap Vinnie in it, speaking as he went.

"Ya see, Vinnie .... what you've gotta learn is .... when you play wi' the big boys, ye have to expect big consequences. Nothing's free, nothing comes without a cost. You wanna watch? Sure, pal, I'll let you watch .... but it'll be from *my* fucking angle, ya ken? *You* don't get to choose the angle!"

Al wrapped him from head to foot, skilfully leaving a small gap for his eyes and mouth so he could still breath. It was done with such precision and expertise, I couldn't help but be engrossed. He'd obviously done it dozens of times before. It was both degrading and comical at the same time. But as much as Vinnie was a complete and utter scumbag who deserved everything he got, I started to feel acutely sorry for him. *No one* should be humiliated like that.

"You're a lucky guy, pal. You've got yourself a right wee darling. Too fucking good for *you*, son, that's for fucking sure! And if you're gonna disrespect her, then *I* am gonna disrespect *you*!"

Vinnie was now completely bound. He looked like a distressed mummy. Then, suddenly, Al reached into his pocket and brought out a Stanley knife! He flicked open the blade and for one terrible, heart-stopping moment I honestly thought he was going to slash him with it. I even ducked in anticipation of the blood about to spurt. Instead he cut the clingfilm from the roll, then proceeded to prod Vinnie in the back with it.

"Bathroom."

Vinnie began to waddle towards the bathroom like a penguin with the runs, with Al behind him prodding him all the way.

"Hey, Bri .... come and watch. You might learn something!"

I didn't want to. I *really* didn't want to. But curiosity got the better of me, even though I was dreading what I might see.

Chloe was waiting with the bath running. When she saw Vinnie she laughed. Al continued to prod him towards the bath which by now was almost full. Vinnie just stood there trembling.

"You two really married?" Al asked Chloe, mock-amazed.

"Yeah."

"What d'ya marry a cunt like *him* for?"

"It was better than college," she said straightforwardly.

Al calmly turned off the taps, then stood eyeball to eyeball with Vinnie who now started to shake violently.

"What ye shaking for, Vinnie? Thought you liked a bit o' violence. A bit o' rough 'n' tumble. A bit o' hitting and hardcore shagging, like. Suddenly gone off the idea, eh? Don't mind it being done to yer wife, though, do ya? Don't mind watching *her* getting hit 'n'

PAINFUL

fucked, right? Well, tough shit, pal! Ya get what ye give in this life!"

Vinnie's eyes were now the size of saucers.

"Bon voyage, ya cunt!"

And he suddenly threw Vinnie into the cold bath. An enormous splash. He went under, emerged again, coughing and spluttering, writhing and gasping for air. It must have been freezing! Chloe smirked.

"There he is, darling – the man of your dreams. The big guy with the big front. He's all yours. Do whatever you want with him. Personally I'd drown the fucker!"

Chloe stared down at Vinnie unemotionally. Then she raised her foot, placed it on his chest, and pushed him under again with a sudden look of hatred and disgust. Vinnie struggled and jerked to no avail. Every time he tried to surface she'd push him down again, holding him under for at least a minute before allowing him to re-emerge. His eyes were bloodshot, his mouth was blue, his entire body was shuddering uncontrollably and he couldn't get his breath. Al was overjoyed.

"Ah, *yeah*! Quality, babe! Congratulations, doll! You've just joined the doms! An' I am now gonna fuck yer brains out! With *your* permission, of course!"

Without waiting for a reply, he lifted her onto the sink.

"'Ey, Vinnie! You wanna watch, right? Here ye go, ma old son! Cop a loada this, ya cunt yeez!"

He pulled down her knickers, grabbed her by her hair, and brought her mouth to his. Chloe's legs opened voluntarily. Al entered easily, and Vinnie watched with his eyes on stalks. It was repellent, riveting and astonishing all at the same time. Al began thrusting and pounding, with Chloe yelling and laughing in defiant bliss. Then Al suddenly broke into song, a loud, raucous version of 'Auld Lang Syne' sung in a thick Glaswegian accent.

"Should auld acquaintance be forgot
And ne'er brought tae mind ....!"

That was my cue to leave. I turned and headed down the hall, stunned, appalled, speechless. And that was the first and last time I would ever attend a fetish party.

22

I was lying on my bed contemplating what life would be like once the plaster casts finally came off. I had an appointment at Sunningdale Park Hospital in two days' time when they would evaluate my recovery and make a decision. They'd either be removed or I'd have to wear them for another few weeks.

To be honest I'd got rather used to them, and was amazed at how adroit I'd become at getting around in them. I'd even given them names – Eric and Ernie. Eric was the one on the right, Ernie the one on the left.

I fantasized about taking up karate, wondered about my golf swing, but my main concern was if I'd be able to walk the same as I did before. I asked Dr Brian Cox, the orthopaedist not the famous TV scientist, that very question at my last follow-up appointment.

"Well, now ...." he deliberated solemnly, ".... that really depends on what sort of walk you have. For example: if you walk like Liam Gallagher, lead singer of Oasis, then probably not. If you skip and hop like the late great Bruce Forsyth, doubtful. But a Prince Charles-type amble, I'd say almost certainly yes."

Morag was now my official housekeeper, doing all the cooking and cleaning and making a very good job of it. She still insisted on wearing her French maid's outfit as it 'put her in the mood'. And Al, true to his word, never went anywhere near her. I sort of missed the screaming though. She would go all lovelorn every time she saw him.

I got to know her pretty well, especially when she was cutting my toenails. She insisted on doing them and I finally succumbed. She was wonderful at it, extremely proficient, and when she'd finished I felt like a new man. And while she was doing it, I learnt her backstory.

She was brought up in Paisley, the 'posh' part of Glasgow, and had a fairly normal middle-class upbringing. She wanted to be a ballerina. Unfortunately she never grew past 4'10", so worked in shoe shops and ladies outfitting before ending up giving cooking lessons to kids with behavioural problems. Of course, she had to taste everything they made and started to put on weight. Then one day she saw Al's ad: 'Attractive Male Seeks Adult Fun', assumed he meant going to the pictures or dining out, so applied. She instantly fell in love with him and they'd been 'together' ever since. Three years in all. She knew about his other women and all the other things he got up to, but she couldn't help herself. He was her 'mon' .... and she'd love him till the day she died. Eat your heart out, Billie Holliday!

I heard a car pulling up outside. I assumed it was Al coming to clear all the rubbish in the driveway, something he'd been avoiding like the plague for over a week now. I then heard the doorbell, which was odd because I'd given him back his key. I presumed he'd forgotten it and Morag would let him in.

I laid back and decided to have a kip. Damn-all else to do. Then, without warning, the bedroom door opened and I felt someone enter. I opened my eyes and there she was – Yvette. Looking stunning.

"Hello, darling," she smiled enticingly.

She was done-up to the nines, hair and makeup immaculate, dressed in her Karen Millen Italian virgin wool overcoat which she loosened and opened immediately to reveal what she was wearing underneath, which just happened to be all the things she

PAINFUL

knew I found irresistible; her De La Vali satin mini dress, chocolate nylon stockings with a seam up the back, and her Christian Louboutin black stiletto heels. She was also wearing the Rina Tairo 18kt woven gold bracelet I bought her as a wedding present, and my favourite perfume (on her, not me), Chanel Coco Mademoiselle. She looked and smelt ravishing. She obviously wanted something.

"Why is all that rubble in the driveway?" she asked as if it was any of her business. "And who's that funny lady with the Scottish accent who let me in?"

"That's Morag, my housekeeper."

"Why is she wearing a French maid's outfit? She looks ridiculous! It's about three sizes too small for her. She's bulging out all over!"

"What do you want, Yvette?" I asked, unimpressed.

"Want? I don't want *anything*, darling. I just came to see how you are. I'm allowed to see how you are, aren't I? I mean, we *are* still married, after all."

She removed her coat and sat on the bed, showing off her gorgeous legs in the chocolate nylon stockings, not to mention the bare cleavage and the voluptuous aroma wafting from her succulent skin.

"So .... how *are* you?" she inquired in her most sexy, alluring voice.

"On the mend," I answered indifferently.

"That's good. I've .... I've really started to miss you."

In spite of myself, I was immediately interested.

"Oh?"

And with that she totally melted. Tears filled her eyes and the helpless, vulnerable Yvette came flooding back.

"Oh, darling, I think I've made the most terrible mistake! I should never have done it! I must have been mad! I don't know what I was thinking! He doesn't *do* anything! Just sits around all day, eating and doing press-ups! I had no idea fitness instructors could be so *lazy*! He has no drive, no ambition. As long as he maintains his stunning physique and ridiculous good looks, he's perfectly happy to live off me .... *and* you!"

She stopped in mid-flow and looked at me in that tender, longing way she always did when she'd seen the error of her ways.

"And you .... you're such a *kind* man." She covered my hand with hers. "You've always been so good to me. Always been there for me. I'm so ashamed of how I've treated you. You don't deserve it. You deserve so much more. Can you ever forgive me?"

"Yes – I forgive you," I uttered quietly.

I didn't mean it but it encouraged her, and she started stroking my hand with her thumb.

"I just want to come back. Forget it ever happened. Show you how sorry I am. Make it up to you in any way I can."

I could feel my resolve dwindling like a wet New Year's resolution.

"It'll never happen again, darling, I promise. Do you believe me?"

"Yes .... I believe you."

"Oh, Brian – I'm going to be such a good wife to you from now on. I've learnt from my mistakes, I really have. I just want to love you .... and care for you .... and be the best wife I can possibly be."

Her hand started to explore my body. I was instant putty. It was pointless resisting. The reverse cowgirl position was inevitable.

23

The next morning she was all over me, even bringing me breakfast in bed – well, Yvette's *idea* of breakfast – lukewarm coffee, burnt toast, and a flower from the garden. But at least she was making the effort, which was nice.

She was wearing the kimono that Morag had borrowed when she'd had a bath. I have to say, it looked somewhat better on Yvette. Of course it helped that she was naked underneath.

She was laughing and bouncing around like an excited child. I'd never seen her so happy. And *so* affectionate, just like she was at the beginning. She kept kissing me and holding me. Then that long loving look into my eyes.

"So …. what do you think? Shall I go and get my things? Move back in?"

I felt slightly awkward. I wasn't completely sure, but I had to admit it *was* nice having her around again. And maybe things *would* be different this time.

"Yes …. go and get your things."

She smiled elatedly, gave me another big kiss, leapt up and began to get dressed.

"But you'll have to get on with Morag," I warned.

I couldn't bear the thought of the two of them at each other's throats. I remember my two sisters constantly bickering and it did my head in.

"Morag?"

"My housekeeper. She's a permanent fixture. She comes in every day."

"I dismissed her."

It stopped me in my tracks.

PAINFUL

"You *what*?"

"Well, yes. She was downstairs, in the way of the toaster actually, so I told her she wouldn't be needed anymore."

"That was a bit presumptuous, wasn't it?"

"There's no point in keeping her, darling .... not if *I'm* here."

"Yvette .... you can't boil an egg!"

"No, but I can put things in the microwave. Order from Deliveroo."

Alarm bells were ringing. Not only did she not consult me about it, we hadn't even discussed her moving back in yet. But that was Yvette. She'd have assumed Jesus had a crush on her. She continued dressing, oblivious.

"Oh, darling .... it's going to be *so* wonderful! I've really learnt from this. I've *grown* from this. I think my life needed this in order for me to expand. To appreciate what I have .... as opposed to craving what I think I want. Does that make sense?"

I nodded, but I didn't really care.

"What about Pedro?"

"Paco."

"Do you still have feelings for him?"

She turned and looked at me with all the heartfelt sincerity of a nun taking her vows.

"No! It's finished! It's over! He's gone! I don't even *like* him. He's a pig! A lazy, narcissistic, self-centred pig!"

She pulled the zip up on her dress.

"I should have known what he was like when he failed to report your accident."

Bang! I wasn't sure if I'd heard her right, but I also knew I had.

"What?"

"Sorry?"

"What did you just say?"

"When?"

"*He failed to report my accident?*"

"Well .... yes. He was in the other car. The one that drove you off the road."

"How do you know?"

"He told me."

"He *told* you? When?"

"The next day." She actually started to look awkward. "But he didn't *know*. He didn't *know* it was you. I mean, it wasn't *deliberate* or anything. It could have been *anyone*. It just happened to be you. One of those .... weird things. One of those strange twists of fate."

It started to come flooding back. The car, the road, the headlights, the tree.

"What car does he drive?"

She looked puzzled by the question.

"Car? Um .... a Mini. A green Mini. Why?"

"I saw it. Straight after the accident. He stopped, saw what had happened, then drove away."

"Exactly. Shows what a horrid person he is!"

"What was he doing on that road, Yvette?"

She went to answer but completely clammed up. She couldn't think of anything.

"He was here, wasn't he? He was here .... with you .... in *my* house. I came back early .... I called you .... you told him to bolt, which is why he was on that road driving like a lunatic. I bet he'd been drinking. Had he been drinking?"

"Well .... he'd had a couple, yes, but I don't think he was ...."

"Then the next day he told you .... he told you he'd run someone off the road .... and your tiny brain worked out it must have been me."

"Yes, but ...."

"He *told* you .... and you still moved in with him."

Her stance became ungainly, her mouth seemed to go dry, and for the first time since I'd known her she appeared to have trouble lying.

"Listen .... let me try and explain. He came here .... I *asked* him to come here .... because I was going to end it. But before I got the chance .... you called and I told him to go because it wouldn't have looked good, would it, him being here when you got back. Then .... when I heard about your accident .... I thought it would be better if I left because I wasn't sure how bad it was .... I mean, you could have been crippled for life .... and .... well, I'm no good at that sort of thing, darling, you *know* I'm not. I'd make a *terrible* nurse! So I left. Yes, it was wrong of me .... I realize that now .... but at the time it seemed like the right thing to do. For *both* of us."

I regarded her coldly.

"Get out, Yvette."

She looked as though she'd been hit by a truck.

"What?"

"Out. Now. Go. And don't come back."

"But .... but *why*? I don't understand. I mean, what's changed?"

"What's *changed*? If you don't know I'm not going to tell you. You're the most shallow person I've ever met. You have the morality of a serial killer. You get your compassion from Poundland. I hope you drown in your own superficiality."

She still looked fairly confused.

"Does that mean I'm not moving back in?"

I almost laughed.

"Yes, Yvette .... that's *exactly* what it means."

She now looked lost.

PAINFUL

"But where am I going to go?"

"How about Brighton? I hear they've got a really good pier you can jump off."

At last it seemed to sink in. There was nothing left to say. She put on her overcoat, stuffed her stockings into the pocket, and slipped into her shoes. She turned to go before thinking of one last parting shot that just might turn it around.

"I still love you, you know."

I looked at her expressionless. All words failed me. The joke was she probably meant it and completely failed to see the irony. I ignored her, she got the hint, and left.

I had a strange, funny, empty feeling as I heard her get in her car and drive away. But more than anything, I felt relieved.

And that was the last time I ever saw Yvette.

24

"There you are, poppet. A nice cup of tea. Milk, a small amount of sugar, not too strong."

Nurse Kimberley. Just as sweet and pretty as I remembered. It was nice to see her again. She made me feel all warm and cosy.

"I bet you're looking forward to having these off," she smiled, referring to the plaster casts.

"It's funny .... I can hardly remember a time when I didn't have them on."

"Let's hope the X-rays look good. Dr Keaton is very thorough."

"Dr Keaton? Where's Dr Cox?"

"Gone."

"Gone? You mean left?"

"Dead."

"*Dead*? No! What happened? Did he get stung by another wasp?"

"Suicide. Threw himself off Beachy Head."

"No! *Why*?"

"No one really knows. He just left a note saying '*Insanity is a state worth striving for*'. He always *was* a bit strange."

The door opened and a woman entered in a white coat, holding my X-rays.

"Brian May?"

She saw me and stopped dead in her tracks.

"Oh, my God!"

"Diane!" I gasped.

"You two know each other?" Kimberly asked innocently.

PAINFUL

"Yes," Diane answered. "We met. Briefly. But it was .... memorable."

"Yes. Memorable," I said in a haze.

"A sort of .... coming together of souls."

"A coming together of souls," I repeated, stunned.

The chemistry was palpable. The moment was electric. Even Kimberley felt it.

"Well .... give me a shout when you want the plaster casts removed."

"*I'll* do it, Kimberley," Diane said pleasantly. "I'm sure you could do with a break."

Kimberley nodded and looked at me knowingly.

"Good luck."

I nodded back and she left. We were alone. I hadn't a clue where I was or what I was saying. I was floating, sinking, levitating, all at the same time.

"Diane. Dr Keaton. Diane Keaton."

"The orthopaedist not the famous Hollywood actress," she smiled.

She had a shine in her eyes and the room lit up.

"So how have you been?" she asked.

I really couldn't think of anything.

"Tortured," I answered.

She laughed sweetly.

"Me too."

She gathered herself.

"Ok. Let's have a look at these legs of yours."

She opened the big envelopes and brought out my X-rays, put them on the screen with the light behind, and studied them with meticulous care.

"Uh-huh. Ah-ha. Oh, yes."

She was just as beautiful and captivating as the first time I saw her. No – *more* so. Because this was without the lights, the music, the dress and the makeup. White coat, flat shoes, day clothes and a small amount of lipstick and mascara. The effect was *startling*. Even the way she examined my X-rays was overwhelming.

"Nice. Gorgeous. Looking good."

Just her voice was enough to make my heart race. And when she stood on her tiptoes to have a closer look at something on the X-ray, I thrilled at her exquisite legs, as if the rest of her wasn't astonishing enough. She finally finished and turned back to me.

"Well .... Mr May .... you've healed brilliantly. I'm impressed. Let's take those bad boys off, shall we?"

She came slowly, seductively towards me, or so I imagined. She put on some disposable gloves like a burlesque dancer getting ready to perform. She produced what looked like a large electric toothbrush with a circular blade on the end.

"This is what we use to cut the plaster. It looks scary but it's not. The blade doesn't spin like a normal saw – it just vibrates back and forth. Completely harmless. Let me show you."

She switched it on. It made a loud noise like a vacuum cleaner.

"I'm going to put it on my hand to show you it doesn't hurt. Okay?"

I nodded helplessly. She put it against her skin without flinching, then turned it off again.

"See? Absolutely painless. Like two submissives meeting at The Skin Club."

She sat on a swivel chair and brought it towards me, a bit like a dentist about to do a filling. She suddenly became more serious.

"You didn't call," she said quietly.

"No," I stuttered. "Your number got smudged by a sexy nurse. First someone spilt drink on it .... then this crazy nurse jumped on me and rubbed herself up against it. It completely disappeared!"

PAINFUL

"I should have written it on your skin," she smiled sensuously.

"But I tried to find you. I tried everything I could think of. I searched and searched. I even advertised on the net."

She looked amused.

"You advertised on the net? What did you say?"

I knew it off by heart.

"'Good looking gentleman would like to reconnect with lady of exotic beauty who gets lonely sometimes. We met at the S and M club last week, you're into K and P, and your favourite restaurant is the Peking Duck in Cobham. If you'd like to carry on from where we left off and join me for a wonderful meal please reply. The man from West Side Story.'"

She looked at me with a mix of pity and delight.

"K and P? What the hell's *that*?"

"K and P. You said you were into K and P."

"*R* and P."

"*R* and P?"

"Restraint and pleasure."

"Ah!" I grasped.

"And my favourite restaurant is The Mandarin Swan in *Chobham*."

"Not the Peking Duck in *Cobham*?"

She shook her head.

"You got your *Cob* and your *Chob* mixed up."

"Not to mention my Duck and my Swan."

"Easily done."

"But it had a fish tank!"

"Well .... sometimes fate plays funny tricks."

"I even went to a fetish party in case you were there."

She laughed affectionately and pushed the hair back from my forehead.

"Oh, darling, that's so sweet!"

And she leant forward and kissed me lightly on the temple.

"I'll get into trouble," she said huskily. "We're not supposed to fraternize with the patients."

She kissed me again then pulled herself together.

"Right – let's get to work!"

She turned on the cutter and began sawing into one of the plaster casts, up and down, in and out. It didn't hurt, but the vibration was intense. And the most embarrassing thing happened – even more embarrassing than treading on popcorn during *Schindler's List* – I got an erection. I was mortified! *And* she noticed!

"Ooh .... you *are* looking forward to getting these off, aren't you, Mr May?" she purred.

PAINFUL

25

Romeo and Juliet fell in love instantly. As did Tony and Maria. Not to mention David Bowie and Iman. It happens. You can't explain it. It makes no sense. But you can't deny it either. The heart thinks quicker than the brain.

I'm a cautious man. I don't rush in easily. I take my time, I weigh things up. Like when I'm investing in a show. But when you know you *know*. Love at first sight. I'd believed in it all my life. And now that I'd found it I wasn't going to let it go.

So I was in the reception area, euphoric and excited, floating on a cloud few men have reached. The plaster casts were off and I'd found my soulmate. My ship had come in. Okay, I still had to wear walking boots – those ugly things you see on skiers who thought they could ski but couldn't – I would have to continue to use crutches for the foreseeable future, as well as facing months of physiotherapy – but this was only a minor irritation. What was concerning me now was Al.

I'd been phoning him for over an hour without a response. Which was unusual. I'd even texted him with no reply. He'd dropped me off at the hospital around noon and returned to the cottage to meet the men who were coming to collect the cement mixer.

I was just about to call for a cab when Diane appeared. I felt a shock at seeing her again. It confirmed that the dream was real. She saw me and smiled.

"Hello, darling ....you still here?"

I found myself babbling rubbish.

"I can't get hold of my .... chauffeur, I suppose you'd call him. Though that's a bit misleading. I mean, he does lots of other things .... not very well, but he *does* them .... and he doesn't look anything *like a* chauffeur. In fact he doesn't look like anything *at all*. He's a bit rough around the edges, know what I mean? Anyway, he's supposed to pick me up but I can't get through to him. I'm starting to become a little concerned."

"Where do you live?"

"Weybridge."

"I'll drive you."

Another shock.

"What?"

"Sure. I've finished for the day, thank God. I've been working all night in A and E. I'm absolutely shattered."

"But you look amazing!"

"You wait till you see me tonight," she winked.

"Tonight?"

"Yes, you're taking me for dinner."

"I am?"

"Only if you want to."

I stared at her in wonder. Thoughts about Al had completely disappeared.

"Anywhere you like. Anywhere in the world! Paris, Rome, Vienna. Just tell me where you want to go and I'll take you!"

"The Mandarin Swan in Fulmer will be fine. Give me five minutes to get my things."

I watched her walk off, thrilled throughout my entire being. Dr Diane Keaton, the orthopaedist not the famous Hollywood actress, was giving me a lift!

26

It was a metallic marina-blue BMW sports convertible, immaculate just like her. Everything about her was immaculate, even the way she drove. Fast but assured.

We talked, but I honestly can't recall much of what was said. I think I told her she was a brilliant driver to which she replied, "I know." I told her a little about Big Al and how I came to meet him. But mostly I just sat there in awe, totally enamoured, besotted, mesmerized, watching everything she did. The way she held the wheel, the way she steered, the way her hands touched the controls, turning down the air-con to a cool 21°. And marvelled at the way that this was actually happening.

By the time we arrived it was starting to get dark. There was a light drizzle. The Ford Sierra was parked in the driveway, but no sign of Al.

"Is that his car?" Diane asked, somewhat surprised.

"Yes. Goes like the clappers, believe it or not."

"He drove you around in *that*?!"

"I told you he wasn't much of a chauffeur."

It all looked quiet and calm. But I still had an uneasy feeling that something wasn't right, though I tried to dismiss it.

"He's probably inside. He has his own key. Probably having a kip knowing him."

I became aware of her watching at me as if studying me.

"So .... see you later?" she asked, looking straight into my eyes.

"I hope so."

"Pick you up around eight?"

"Yes, please."

"You've *definitely* got my number this time."

"In my phone."

"Do you want me to help you inside?"

"Good lord, no! I'm ready to bop the night away!"

"Can't wait," she said in a low, beguiling voice.

She leaned across and we kissed, a full on-the-mouth kiss that seemed to go on forever.

"This *is* real, isn't it?" I asked in a stupor.

"Yes, darling – it's real."

I got out of the car, waved and blew her a kiss as I watched her zoom off like a boy racer.

I turned and headed slowly towards the cottage. I had to go gingerly because the pain killers were starting to wear off. Then halfway up the drive I spotted something on the ground. I stopped and looked. A mobile. Smashed. It was his. I looked around, alarmed.

"Al?"

I then saw a body lying prone in the rubble. It wasn't moving.

"Al!"

I went as fast as I could towards it. It was him. My breath stopped, my mouth went dry. He was soaking wet and covered in blood. His jaws were slack, his face was drained of colour. He looked dead.

"Oh, my God!"

I didn't know what to do. I instinctively reached for my mobile and called Diane. Luckily she answered immediately.

"Can you come back? There's been an accident. I think he's dead!"

I ended the call and turned back to Al. He still wasn't moving. Devoid of ideas, I let go of the crutches and fell to my knees, yelling as I landed. It hurt like hell! I recovered and felt his pulse. There was nothing. I panicked and cried out.

"Oh, no! Oh, no!"

Big Al McFadden. People like Big Al McFadden aren't supposed to die, they're supposed to live forever. Stand in the middle of a war zone and emerge unscathed. I became emotional and started talking to him as if he could hear me. From what I can remember, it was complete and utter gibberish.

"Listen .... you're not going to believe this .... but I've found her! Diane. Roman goddess of the moon! She's a doctor! A doctor at the hospital! Can you believe that? She did my legs! She did my legs and .... she remembered me. She *remembered* me, Al! She remembered me and .... we're having dinner tonight and .... and ...."

And suddenly I broke down. Completely overwrought. And I found myself crying like a baby.

"Al .... I'm sorry! I'm *so* sorry! I know we had our ups and downs .... I slagged you off a few times .... but you were there for me. You were *always* there for me! I didn't want it, I didn't ask you to be, you kind of *insisted* on it. But I couldn't have got through it without you. It was a truly unforgettable experience. And I'll never regret hiring you for nothing. Even if it *did* cost me an absolute fortune!"

All of a sudden I heard a long, loud passing of wind. I was stunned. It *couldn't* be – could it? Yes – it was him! I recognized it from our night at The Dog And Ferret. I stared at him in wonder and awe. I'd never been so happy to hear something that disgusting!

"Al! Al! You're alive!"

He slowly opened his eyes and spoke faintly.

"I fucking hope so – some bird has answered ma advert."

His voice was weak but still full of spirit.

"What happened?"

"Those cunts .... those cunts wi' the cement mixer .... they came back 'n' beat the shit outa us. They wanted two and a half k. Two and a half fucking k for six weeks hire. Sixty quid a day. I told 'em to do one. Next thing I know, one hits me over the head with a crowbar, the other starts destroying ma legs wi' a fucking baseball bat. I musta passed out with the pain."

"Can you walk?"

"Ah cannae move! Ma knees are smashed to fuck! Ma head feels like it's gone AWOL!"

Thankfully I heard Diane's car return. She screeched to a halt and came running towards us like the leading lady in an action film.

"It's okay .... he's not dead!" I called on seeing her.

She kneeled the other side of him and began inspecting his injuries.

"Nasty head wound."

"It's his legs. He said he can't move them."

"Does this hurt?" she asked him as she manipulated one of them.

He let out the loudest prolonged scream I'd ever heard. It sounded like he was being stretched on the rack.

"Right. I'll call for an ambulance."

She stood up and brought out her phone with Al immediately protesting.

"No! No! No ambulance!"

She studied him, baffled.

"Why not?"

"No ambulance, no hospital!"

"Don't be ridiculous. You've lost a lot of blood. You'll need stitches. Your legs need to be X-rayed, you've possibly got multiple fractures ...."

PAINFUL

"I dinnae care! I'm no going to hospital an' that's final!"

Diane turned to me to make sense of it.

"What's wrong with him?"

I felt I needed to be on the same level to explain it.

"Do you think you could help me up, please, darling?"

"Oh – yes – of course."

She got me to my feet with the skill of a physiotherapist and handed me my crutches.

"So what is it? What's his problem?"

I struggled slightly. It was hard to find the right words. It sounded so absurd.

"He doesn't exist."

She stared at me blankly.

"Sorry?"

"There are no records of him. No stamps, no passport, no bank account. He doesn't exist."

"How can he *not exist*?"

I cleared my throat.

"He's an escaped convict."

"Aye!" Al suddenly yelled. "An' I'm no going back there! No fucking way! It's no fit for a starving cat! I'd rather lose both legs an' have ma knob chopped off!"

"Oh, shut up, you stupid man!" Diane said sharply as she dialled 999. "You're going!"

27

We followed the ambulance back to Sunningdale Park Hospital where Al was rushed into A and E. We both hung around while he was attended to, thus missing our dinner date. But it didn't matter. It was still wonderful. We had cheese sandwiches and coffee from the vending machine. It was ridiculously romantic.

I found out more about her. She was 40, she'd been on her own for six years, choosing her work and independence over someone else's needs. She'd been horribly hurt when she was younger, though she didn't go into details. But she openly admitted to having trust issues. That was one of the things I loved about her – her honesty. She never once tried to hide.

I discovered it had been her one and only time at The Skin Club. She'd heard about it from someone at the hospital, one of the cleaners believe it or not, who was into that sort of thing. And, like myself, she went out of curiosity.

"And R 'n' P?"

She laughed.

"Restraint and pleasure. She told me about that too. *And* sub 'n' dom. I just said it to sound good. Like I knew what I was talking about. I've never done anything like it in my life."

"*Would* you?"

She looked straight at me.

"Maybe. With the right person."

We stared at each other, no words necessary.

Al had thirty-seven stitches in his head and external fixation devices on both legs. He'd be out of action for

PAINFUL

at least three months. The only thing that calmed him down was a promise that I'd pay for him to go private, thus avoiding anyone checking his NHS contributions which were zilch. When they asked him his name he told them it was Ronald McDonald.

I couldn't help but chuckle with the irony of it. There he was, both legs in traction, two black eyes, bruises everywhere, and totally reliant on everyone around him. A complete role-reversal.

Around 10 he was moved to the Churchill Suite. Diane offered to give me another lift home, then just as we were about to leave, there was suddenly a commotion. Some sort of panic going on in one of the rooms. There was a loud beeping sound, like an alarm. A nurse came running out looking scared. She darted into another room and returned almost immediately with a defibrillator on wheels which she pushed back into the Churchill Suite at full pelt. A doctor and several nurses appeared and rushed after her. I don't know how, but I knew it was for him. Diane told me to stay put and followed.

25 minutes later she returned and told me he was dead. An undetected skull fracture causing internal bleeding and brain damage leading to cardiac arrest. Or I *think* that's what she said. All I could hear was this loud buzzing noise like you get when you're about to faint.

It was nonsensical. He'd been sitting up and moaning about not being able to have a fag just an hour before.

We sat down and she held my hand. She explained they'd tried everything. They tried for twenty minutes but nothing worked. He just wouldn't come round. My first thought was I'd have to tell Morag.

28

How do you organize a funeral for someone who doesn't exist? It's not easy, I can tell you! I didn't know where he was from, who his next of kin was, I wasn't even sure of his real name. The death certificate said Ronald Macdonald. I announced it in The Guardian, The Glasgow Herald and Loot, and hoped for the best.

It also brought up some strange thoughts and feelings, mainly the absurdity and pointlessness of it all. All those years of paying into the system, all that stress we have about finding a job, paying our bills, making sure we have enough stamps, insurance policies, pensions, wills, mortgages, retirement schemes. Then we stop breathing and what's it all been for? Ultimately *none* of us exist. When did that get so complicated?

Morag, of course, was inconsolable.

"Ah knew it!" she wailed. "Ah *knew* something like this was gunna happen! Ah knew he'd get his comeuppance! Ah could see it coming a mile off! Ye cannae play with fire without getting yer bottom hairs singed!"

I explained it was nothing to do with the S and M, it was a dispute over the cement mixer, but she didn't seem to take it in.

"He was coming up fur sixty, fur god's sake! Ah told him, I sez, yer too old fur all this gallivanting, Ally! Weed, booze, coke – it's time ya settled doon! But diddy listen? Did he chuckie, the stubborn wee eejit!"

They got the guys that did it. Irish gypsies – sorry – *travellers*. Presumably they took the cement mixer around with them.

PAINFUL

Slough crematorium. A Friday. Scheduled to start at 11.30. Seating for 150. By 11.25 there were three of us – me, Diane and Morag who was already bawling her eyes out. Some old bloke at the back working the CD player. The ceremony was supposed to last 45 minutes but I could see it being over in five.

Then at 11.27 there was suddenly an influx. People in bondage gear, about twenty of them. Rubber hoods, blindfolds, harnesses, Venetian face masks, someone in a gas mask, all dressed outlandishly. A couple of police women, the scantily clad variety, with truncheons and handcuffs. And among them, to my alarm, was Vendetta, dressed as she was before in her red PVC dress with a split up the middle, red platform boots to match, and the same scary vamp-like makeup and hair. She was leading some poor bloke on a chain with a collar round his neck. It was Keith on a leash. Completely naked apart from his leather codpiece. Not exactly appropriate for a funeral, I thought, but at least it was black. Then to my horror, he/she/it suddenly stopped and stared down at me.

"Don't I know you from somewhere?" it said in that deep, masculine, formidable voice.

I decided to play dumb.

"Me? No. Absolutely not. I haven't been to the circus in years."

"You ever go down The Skin Club?"

"The Skin Club? What's that, some sort of nudist camp, is it? No, I'm not into that sort of thing, I'm afraid. Like to keep my privates .... *private* .... if you know what I mean."

It thought about it for a second, then yanked the chain and pulled Keith over to the other side where it made him sit on the floor and lick its boots.

A minute later a woman appeared with a long line of kids trailing behind her. I counted ten of them, aged anywhere between eighteen all the way down to a baby of about 6 months who she was holding in her arms. All had flaming ginger hair, apart from one, a pretty little black boy of about six who seemed to stand out from the others for his sweet face and mild demeanour. All the rest were pulling each other's hair or punching each other, mainly ignored by the woman, though every now and then she'd clump one of them round the head. She was in an old, rather tatty overcoat with no makeup and her hair in urgent need of a salon. Rough beyond belief. I don't think she had any teeth. She scowled around angrily, then made them all sit three rows from the front, taking up the entire bench. The minute she sat down she unbuttoned her blouse and began breastfeeding.

Then just when I thought the coffin was about to enter, Steve arrived, coked out of his head. I knew the signs by now, especially the white powder around his nose and upper lip. A dead giveaway.

"Oi – raspberry!"

I cringed. He came and sat with us in the front row.

"Is he here yet?"

"Does it *look* like he's here?!" I said, raising my eyes to heaven.

He turned his attention to Diane, especially her legs.

"Alright, darling? How do *you* know the deceased, then?"

"I'm supporting Brian."

"*Brian?*" he chortled, amused. "That old cunt? What you supporting *him* for? He gets *enough* support from fucking Andrew Lloyd Webber!"

PAINFUL

Suddenly a loud guitar chord struck up, followed by two thumps on a snare drum. Everyone stood up respectfully as Big Al's body was brought in to the tune of 'Jailhouse Rock' by Elvis, Morag's choice. The pallbearers looked a bit bemused, though one of them had the quiff and sideburns.

"The warden threw a party in the county jail
The prison band was there and they began to wail ...."

They carried the coffin to the front and laid it down while Elvis continued to rock in his cell.

"Number 47 said to number 3
You're the cutest jailbird I ever did see ...."

Steve, sensitive soul that he is, leaned across Diane to have a word with me.

"'Ere, Brian – I've got a brilliant business proposition for you!"

I gritted my teeth.

"For god's sake, Steve, not *now*! The eulogy is about to start!"

"Who's doing it?"

"*I* am."

He looked dumbfounded.

"But you're as boring as fuck!"

"Everybody in the whole cell block
Was dancin' to the Jailhouse Rock!"

The song ended. Everyone sat down. There was a small silence, some clearing of throats, then I stood up, went onto the raise, and stood behind a small lectern with my pathetic scribbled notes. I was as nervous as hell. I took in the number of people, all of them staring straight at me, waiting for me to say something clever or profound. Even the woman and her kids had gone silent. I spoke into the microphone.

PAINFUL

"Big Al McFadden .... sometimes known as Ronald McDonald .... what can one say about Big Al McFadden? I have to admit, I spent an awful long time trying to think of something. A charismatic clown, an enigmatic villain, larger than life. A huge character that dominated every room he entered .... *literally*. Since his untimely death ten days ago, I've discovered things about him that have shed a whole new light on his life and character, thanks mainly to his partner of three years .... Morag Platt."

"Slut! Filthy slut!" shouted the woman with the ten kids in a thick Glaswegian accent.

I tried to ignore her.

"For example – he was a big Elvis fan. Hence his entrance to the tune of *Jailhouse Rock*. Appropriate in more ways than one. And, even more amazingly, did you know he was once the lead singer of a punk band called Sid Scrotum And The Foreskins? They even made a record – a delightful little ditty entitled 'Shut Yer Gob Before I Smack It' which was a minor hit, getting to number 48 in the charts. Unfortunately they couldn't follow it up, the record company dropped them, and the manager ran off with all the royalties."

"Bollocks!" shouted the woman again. "Loada bollocks! They played one gig at a pub in Renfrew an' got booed off the stage!"

I referred to my notes and tried to continue as best I could.

"But there *was* a softer side to Al, as demonstrated when he used to speak about his dog Jock, a homeless mongrel who he found on the street and took home to look after."

"That's bollocks an' aw! There was naw dog called Jock! He made all that up! The nearest he got to a dog

PAINFUL

was that fat fucking shag-bucket sitting in the front!" the woman screamed.

It was pointless continuing with the notes, which were obviously wildly way-off. I decided to discard them and go with a more 'informal' type of service.

"Perhaps *you'd* like to say a few words, Mrs .... um ...." I said to her as she continued to breastfeed. "You seem to know an awful lot about him."

"Aye – ah *should* – ah was his bloody wife!"

Me and my notes came to a screeching halt.

"His *wife*?!"

Morag now stood up, bawling her eyes out.

"No! No!"

"Aye! Aye!" yelled the woman standing up to confront her, the baby still sucking on one of her nipples.

A shouting match ensued across the aisles.

"But he was ma mon! He was ma mon an' ah was his burd!"

"Aye, when he wasnae coming up tae Glesgae tae rump the arse offa *me*!"

"No! No!"

"Aye! Aye!"

She now turned to address the entire congregation.

"Ten kids! Ten bloody kids! All his! And he never paid a bloody penny towards 'um!"

She sat down again, satisfied with her declaration of downtrodden abandonment. The sweet little black boy just sat there amongst all the others, ultra-meek, still none the wiser as to who his real father might be. I stared around with everyone staring dumbly back at me. Even the bondage lot seemed lost for words.

"Does .... anyone else want to say something?"

"Aye!" cried the woman, now in full flow. "His eldest son Dennis would like tae say a word!"

She turned to Dennis encouragingly.

"Up yeez go, son."

Dennis got up, full of teenage angst and acne, the most ginger of them all, and made his way up to the podium. He had that look of neanderthal brawn and no brain. I moved to one side to allow him to speak. He reached the microphone. Everyone was silent.

"Cunt!" he suddenly said. "He was a cunt! An oot 'n' oot cunt! He ne'er did *nothin'* fur me or ma maw! Ah hardly ever fucking *saw* him! Not even on ma fucking birthday! Didn't even share his fucking drugs! He was a cunt! An oot 'n' oot cunt!"

Everyone watched in open-mouthed disbelief as Dennis, his spots as angry as his outburst, went back to his seat to be patted on the head by his 'maw'.

"Well done, son!" she beamed proudly.

And that was it. There seemed little point in continuing. No one else wanted to speak and I'd run out of courage. Morag was meant to read a poem but she was in such a state I knew she'd never get through it.

"Well .... I suppose we might as well .... end the proceedings .... and send him on his way."

I nodded to the bloke at the back who pressed some button and the coffin moved forward on a motorized conveyor belt to be burned to a cinder. The curtains closed and Al disappeared to the tune of 'You Ain't Nothing But A Hound Dog', again Morag's choice. I'd have chosen something a little softer, but she said it was his favourite. I went back to my seat with Diane now consoling Morag who was sobbing into a box of Kleenex.

And suddenly Big Al McFadden was no more. Gone. Just like that. No more S 'n' M, no more advertising in Loot, hiding from the bacon. Just gone. Hopefully to that great Skin Club in the sky – though I sort of

PAINFUL

doubted it. The service that I thought might only last five minutes actually lasted for ten.

We all stood up, people started to leave, I gathered my crutches and was about to follow when Steve prodded me on the shoulder. I turned back.

"A mobile dungeon," he said.

I blinked and stood for a moment, trying to absorb this bizarre piece of information.

"*What*?!"

"A mobile dungeon. Great business opportunity. Can't fail. There's already one operating in Bradford. It was on the telly last week. All you need is a van with a dungeon in the back, a few instruments of torture .... you know .... whips, handcuffs, chains .... just drive round the estates offering a bit of flogging 'n' bondage, fifty quid a pop .... it's a winner!"

I told him to try Andrew Lloyd Webber.

29

That night Diane and I finally made it to The Mandarin Swan in Chobham. It was everything I hoped it would be. Small and intimate, warm and welcoming, exquisite food, and a beautiful tropical fish tank with fish that were actually *alive.* The lighting was soft and flattering, and Diane had never looked more radiant.

We'd hardly seen each other. She'd been working long shifts at the hospital, I'd been busy organizing the funeral, and though I felt I'd known her forever, this was actually the first time we'd been out just the two of us. Our first official date!

People react to death in different ways. I'd gone through the grief and shock, the stress of the funeral service, and now all I wanted to do was celebrate, not just Al's life but my own. To that end, I ordered one bottle of wine after another, drank far too quickly, and before I knew it my mouth had got completely confused with my brain. I suddenly told her I loved her.

There was a silence. She seemed taken aback, almost shocked. It wasn't the reaction I expected. She lowered her eyes, pensive.

"Brian .... there's something I have to tell you ...."

Oh, no. I immediately feared the worst. My face fell, my heart stopped.

"You're married."

"No."

"There's someone else."

"No."

"You're a lesbian."

"I can't have children."

I was stunned. It took me completely by surprise. I wasn't sure how to respond. Not because I didn't empathize, but because I'd never thought of it as being a game-changer. Like the insensitive insular berk I'd always been, I'd never put myself in that place. It just hadn't occurred to me it could be an issue.

"It's the regret of my life," she said softly. "It never leaves. It's with me everywhere."

"How did you find out?"

"First real relationship .... early twenties .... we met at med school. Fell madly in love, got married. Blissful for a time. Love's young dream an' all that. Everything new and exciting. Then it all changed. I got pregnant. And he became someone else. Started hitting me. Shouting at me. Belittling me. For no reason. If there wasn't a reason he'd find one. His food wasn't cooked right, I hadn't paired his socks correctly, I'd said something wrong in front of his friends. He became convinced I was having an affair and the baby wasn't his. He'd pull my hair and try to get me to admit it. Then one night he accused me of flirting with someone at a restaurant. I didn't even know who he was talking about. He pinned me against a wall and punched me so hard in the stomach I thought I was going to die. I started to bleed. And I lost the baby. Six months pregnant. A beautiful little girl. He wouldn't even let me ring for an ambulance. I had to miscarry in the bathroom."

She paused, trying to contain her emotions.

"A few months later I went to a gynaecologist and was told I had 'premature ovarian failure'. Do you know what that is?"

I shook my head.

"The ovaries stop functioning normally which leads to infertility. I came home desolate. I didn't even tell him.

PAINFUL

I hated his guts by then. Thankfully he left soon after. Had an affair with some bimbo and moved in with her. But it rather put me off men. For a long time. I couldn't bear anyone coming near me. Then .... for some reason .... I started sleeping around. A different one every night. I still don't know why. I'd go down some club and pull the first man I saw. Take them home, kick them out in the morning. It didn't matter who. Any stranger would do. The more dangerous and sordid the better. It was almost like a punishment. I wanted to be harmed, abused. But I soon realized that wasn't the answer. There *was* no answer. Only me – learning to live with myself. And that's what I've been doing .... living with myself. Privately, alone. And most of the time it's okay. But every now and then that shadow falls."

I wanted to hold her. My heart hurt along with hers. I felt her pain.

"I've had a few relationships .... but nothing meaningful. Nothing really stuck."

She now looked at me with those dark, deep, mesmerizing eyes that I'd found enthralling from the moment we'd met.

"So there you go. There's the regret. I can't have children. I'm sorry." She managed to smile. "Shame you don't have any."

It was the saddest smile I'd ever seen.

"What about me? Will *I* stick?"

She now became warm and affectionate again, putting her hand over mine.

"Yes. Of *course.* You *have.*"

"We could adopt," I suddenly said.

Her eyes melted, her pain softened.

"Yes. We could. And by the way – I love you too."

PAINFUL

It was one of those amazing one-off moments you never forget and want to celebrate for the rest of your life. 9.48 on a Friday night in one of the nicest restaurants I'd ever been to. I went hell for leather and ordered another bottle of wine.

"We'll have to get a cab," I beamed, slurring slightly.
"What for?" she answered, all innocence.
"Well .... we've both had rather a lot to drink."
"Yes, but I only live round the corner in the village. Just a five minute walk from here."
"But what about me?"
"*You*? You're staying with me."
"I *am*?"
Our eyes locked together.
"Only if you want to, that is."
"Oh – oh, yes – I'd really like that."
"I mean, there's a very nice spare room, if you'd prefer," she said playfully.
"No – no, your bed will be fine."

30

Everything was new. Her skin, her body, her smell. Her hair, her mouth, her taste. The way she felt. All amazing and new.

I went under the covers and explored her nakedness. I began to kiss and worship every inch of her. From her feet, all the way up her legs to her inner thighs, finally arriving at the altar of her femininity. A sacred realm of lost lovers and intimate strangers. It tasted sweet and delectable. I heard her start to moan, quietly at first, gradually getting louder. I stayed there for as long as it took to satisfy her. Then, when I knew she was fulfilled, I went to her belly-button and licked it. Then her entire stomach, then her firm beautiful breasts. Her shoulders and neck. Then her mouth again. And there she was, blindfolded, both hands tied to each side of the bed, powerless, exposed. I removed the blindfold and stared into her eyes.

"Was that ok, darling?"

"Oh, *yes*!" she purred.

"Is that R 'n' P?"

She nodded, stretched luxuriously, and breathed out a long sigh of contentment and relief.

"Yes, darling – that's R 'n' P."

EPILOGUE

A year later Yvette gave me a 'quickie' divorce for a large sum of money and Diane and I were married. And a year after that she gave birth to a beautiful baby boy, a miracle child. He had brilliant blonde locks and big blue eyes. We named him Henry, but I called him 'Choochie' because he was so cute and sweet.

I now view life as a long, erratic game of golf on a course of someone else's choosing. Sometimes you're in a bunker, sometimes you're in the rough, sometimes your swing is off, your chipping's all to cock, and you keep losing your balls. But every now and then you hit that one, incredible shot-in-a-million that flies off the tee, lands on the green, and rolls effortlessly into the hole. *Mostly*, of course, you're just happy to be out there playing.

PAINFUL

'Fear knocked, love answered, and no one was there.'

PAINFUL

Printed in Great Britain
by Amazon